The horses stampeded down from the hills. What could they be running from? Had fire burned into a canyon where they'd been grazing?

The golden-brown horse was the Phantom's lead mare. Usually, she controlled the herd while the silver stallion watched from above, or hung back where he could see his entire band. But where was he now?

Sam could barely see the herd. Dark smoke reduced the mustangs to shadows darting and stumbling in the direction of the captive horses.

Suddenly a whirlwind of movement swept through the milling herd.

Glinting brightly through the smoke, the Phantom galloped downhill. He ignored the worn path, leaping sharp turns to make his own way, rushing to take charge of his band.

Read all the books about the

Phantom Stallion

Phantom Stallion

∞ 16 ∞
The Wildest Heart

TERRI FARLEY

AVON BOOKS

An Imprint of HarperCollins*Publishers*

Library of Congress Catalog Card Number:
2004095711
ISBN 0-06-058317-7

First Avon edition, 2005

❖

Visit us on the World Wide Web!
www.harperchildrens.com

N
NW NE
W E
SW SE
S

WILD HORSE
VALLEY

THREE PONIES
RANCH

DEERPATH
RANCH

RIVER BEND
RANCH

GOLD DUST
RANCH

WAR DRUM
FLATS

ARROYO
AZUL

ALKALI

WILLOW SPRINGS
WILD HORSE
CENTER

LOST CANYON

Chapter One ⌖

$\mathcal{S}$weat dripped into Samantha Forster's eyes.

She blinked furiously, but it didn't help. Her eyes still burned. Looking down past her cut-off jeans, she saw that her tanned legs were marked with smears of red-brown paint. When she tossed her head to fling back the bangs stuck to her forehead, she stumbled on a pebble and tripped.

"Ow!" She might as well howl her discomfort. No one was around to hear.

This had sounded like such a good idea a couple of days ago.

Blind Faith Mustang Sanctuary had hundreds of acres of fenced land that bordered wild horse country. Mrs. Allen, the sanctuary's owner, was a softhearted but particular woman, and she wanted her miles of board fence painted to match her redwood barn.

Sam had known she'd have to work hard, but Mrs. Allen had tempted her with exciting possibilities. With wild horses inside the fence and wild horses outside the fence and Sam in the middle, who knew what wonderful things could happen?

Besides, she'd be doing a good deed.

She knew darn well she should store up good deeds and make sure Dad, Gram, and her stepmother Brynna noticed, because horses got her into trouble. She didn't plan it that way, it just kept happening.

This chore couldn't possibly get her in trouble. She had a week off from working in the Horse and Rider Protection program and she knew how to paint, so she'd snapped up the chance to help Mrs. Allen.

It wasn't all fussiness, either. By next summer, Mrs. Allen hoped to have the ranch so tidy and organized, people would drive from all over the country to see mustangs living as they were supposed to—wild and free. The only difference between her horses and those of the surrounding range was that these mustangs would have died if Mrs. Allen hadn't saved them.

Trudy Allen had adopted fourteen captive mustangs. One had malformed legs. Another was blind. The rest were old or unbeautiful. All had been declared "unadoptable."

Mrs. Allen had taken them in before they could

be destroyed and she'd turned Deerpath cattle ranch into a place where horses ran free.

She deserved Sam's help.

Besides, Sam thought, gazing over her shoulder toward the Calico Mountains, she'd seen the Phantom here several times.

If the silver stallion, who'd once been her hand-raised colt, sensed she was here and alone, he might come to her.

Sam had a lot of good reasons to happily tackle her chore. But it was still July in Nevada's high desert. And it was really hot.

Sam lifted the hem of her T-shirt, then stopped.

She'd been about to blot the sweat from her eyes, but forget it. Her red T-shirt sagged with the same steamy dampness of a saddle blanket after a hard ride.

She'd never minded it before. You just lifted off the saddle and when you raised the saddle blanket, it was like the horse had been in a sauna. But she didn't want to put such sogginess on her face.

Sam smiled at the image of her bay gelding Ace in a sauna.

The best thing about working alone was that no one would hear her silly thoughts. Not even Ace.

For the last two mornings, Sam had ridden Ace to Mrs. Allen's house, then said a prayer for her own safety as she climbed into Mrs. Allen's tangerine-colored pickup truck for a ride out to the section of fence she'd be painting.

She didn't really mind sharing the front seat with Imp and Angel, two Boston bull terriers who bounced on her lap as if they hadn't noticed she'd taken their usual place in the truck. It was Mrs. Allen who scared her.

Mrs. Allen might be the worst driver in the world. She pressed her foot to the floor, accelerating over sagebrush, down gullies, and up rocky side hills. Instead of staring through the windshield to see where she was going, she usually turned to Sam and kept up a running conversation.

The first rough drive from the ranch house and saddle horse corral out to the raw wood fence had resulted in paint cans popping open and spewing paint all over the bed of her truck.

Once they'd reached their destination and started to unload, both Sam and Mrs. Allen had been surprised.

"Looks like there's been a massacre," Mrs. Allen had grumbled.

Since then, she'd insisted the unopened paint cans be left along the fence line.

"That way we don't have to haul them out with you," Mrs. Allen had said, quite pleased with her solution, but something about the idea made Sam uneasy.

Coo, coo. Sam looked over each shoulder.

She heard the dove, but saw nothing alive. No birds, no antelope, no wild horses. Only yellow cheatgrass moved, blowing in the wind.

Sam looked up into a blueberries-and-cream sky. That dove was calling from somewhere.

"I don't know about this," Sam said to the invisible bird. "Leaving these paint cans out overnight just doesn't seem like a good idea. Not that I think a coyote is going to pry off a lid and lap it up."

Oh well, Mrs. Allen had lived on this ranch longer than Sam had been alive. She probably knew what she was doing.

Sam stroked a smooth swathe of paint over the next board just as the wind gusted, singing through her little gold hoop earrings. Sam angled her body to keep the wind from spraying dust into the wet paint.

She watched for bumps and black flecks to appear, but they didn't.

Sam nodded with satisfaction, then thought, *Great. My big thrill for the day is watching paint dry.*

Sam dipped her brush and swabbed another red-brown stripe on the boards.

If her best friend Jen Kenworthy had been free to help, this wouldn't be so boring. But Jen's mother had drafted her to cook all week.

Haying crews would be coming to work on their ranch soon. Unlike Gram, Jen's mom, Leah, didn't enjoy making meals for dozens of hungry men. Leah's solution was to do everything ahead.

Jen was stuck inside the kitchen of the foreman's house on Gold Dust Ranch, chopping vegetables, browning beef, and kneading pillows of dough into loaves. All week, she'd help cook up soups, stews, and mountains of bread to fill the freezers at the Gold Dust Ranch.

Linc Slocum, the richest man in northern Nevada and the owner of Gold Dust Ranch, had actually offered to have meals for the haying crew catered.

"Mom was tempted," Jen had told Sam, "But she ended up reminding him that the closest restaurant is Clara's coffee shop in Alkali and Clara doesn't do takeout, especially out to the alfalfa fields."

The thought of Clara's made Sam draw a deep breath. Dad was taking the family out to dinner at Clara's. Tonight.

Dinner out on a weekend would be unusual, but a restaurant meal on a Tuesday was downright abnormal.

Something was up, and she'd find out what tonight. The last time Dad had made dinner into a special event had been last fall, when he had announced his engagement to Brynna Olson.

Sam felt impatient, but she guessed she could wait until tonight to learn why Dad, Gram, and Brynna had been acting so weird.

Not *bad* weird, Sam thought, picking a paintbrush bristle from the fresh paint. Giddy and mysterious weird.

A neigh, reduced by distance to a whisper, floated across the sanctuary pastures. Sam recognized it as a challenge and she'd bet it came from Roman.

Sam shaded her eyes, but she could only count seven of Mrs. Allen's wild horses.

That dark blob was probably Roman. Even from here, he seemed to strut. The liver chestnut gelding with the extreme Roman nose thought he was in charge of the captive herd. Now, he stood guard over the adopted mustang mares with foals.

Sam smiled. Though Roman stayed far out in the pasture, some of the other horses grazed near enough to see clearly. She could see a black mare who'd been deemed unadoptable because she was old and mean. She didn't look cranky now. Ears she'd once pinned back in bad temper tilted forward in motherly curiosity toward her bright bay colt. Mrs. Allen had named the mare Licorice and her foal Windfall.

Grazing beside Licorice was the yellow dun mare Mrs. Allen had adopted last. The mare's name was Fourteen, because Mrs. Allen had decided adopting thirteen horses that had been slated for euthanasia was unlucky, and picked one more. Fourteen had given birth to a dorsal-striped filly that looked like one of the primitive horses Sam had seen daubed on the stone tunnel leading to the Phantom's hidden valley.

Belle and Faith were closest to Sam.

"Faith!" Sam called for about the tenth time. "Here, baby!"

But "baby" wouldn't come. The Medicine Hat filly

was nearly a yearling. Lanky and almost full-grown, Faith had kept her palomino pinto coloring and sassy attitude. Now she twitched her tail and ignored Sam, just as she had all day.

Remembering the snowy night she, Jen, Jake, and half the cowboys in the county had gone searching for the blind foal, Sam wondered if Faith shouldn't show a little gratitude.

But she only wondered for a minute. Really, she was glad for Faith.

Pastured on hundreds of acres that rolled from the La Charla River to the edge of wild horse country, the filly wasn't hampered by her blindness. She was as wild as any member of the Phantom's herd, with no need of humans. More than any of the other captive horses, she dismissed the calls of people as she might the cawing of crows.

Sam was wiping her forearm across her brow, when all the captive mustangs suddenly quit grazing. Some heads came up slowly, grass falling from their lips. Other heads jerked up and the horses backed in surprise.

Sam heard something, too, but what was it?

Not the coo of a dove or the distant rush of traffic on the highway. It was almost like sand, sifting away from some disturbance. Sam turned around slowly.

Ghostly pale, the Phantom stood alone on the brow of a hill.

For an instant, he held his head high and his nostrils flared. The stallion drew in the hundreds of scents on the wind. His neck lengthened, showing the silver dapples along his throat. His hooves danced restlessly in place.

It must be confusing, Sam thought. Wind swirled nearby scents and faraway ones, all together. He'd smell her, the captive mustangs, the unfamiliar scent of paint, the chalk-dry dirt and sagebrush under his hooves, and maybe even a drop of juice on her hand from the apple she'd fed Ace this morning.

Sam took a quick look around. She knew she was alone, but she had to be certain.

"Zanzibar!" She pronounced the stallion's secret name in three slow syllables.

This time, she didn't whisper.

At once, the stallion's gray-edged ears flicked forward, homing in on that name only the two of them knew. The stallion's head lifted higher. A nicker rode the wind to Sam.

Our magic has two halves, Sam thought. She spoke the first word of the charm and the silver stallion answered.

He stood like polished ivory, content, this time, to let the spell be shared silence. Not a romp or a ride, Sam thought, just stillness she mirrored by barely breathing.

Suddenly, another sound made the stallion's ears flick right, then left.

Sam couldn't hear anything, but the Phantom gave a snort. Then, head lurching forward, legs reaching, tail streaming like a silken banner, the stallion leaped into a gallop.

Take me with you.

It wasn't a wish that made Sam yearn after him, it was an instinct.

She knew better than to want him for her own. But she felt—Sam shook her head. She looked down at her dirty hands, imagining she was that girl who'd seen the first wild horse running, thousands of years ago.

Destined to drudgery, to hauling water and firewood, tending younger children and cleaning out the cave, she would have run after such beauty.

Wow, and once she'd captured the wild horse, then tamed and ridden him, there would have been no stopping her.

Half-hypnotized by the stallion's appearance, Sam started to rub the goose bumps from her arms, before remembering she still held her paintbrush. She dropped it.

The brush lay flat on the ground. She could only guess what a gooey, gritty mess the other side would be. Last night, Mrs. Allen had made her rinse the paintbrush until no barn red remained on the black bristles. It took forever and she hated the gasoline-like smell of paint thinner. Now, she'd have to use it twice as long.

At least she had another brush. Sam reached into the back pocket of her cut-offs and took out the spare brush Mrs. Allen had made her bring.

She'd only been using it a few minutes when she heard an engine's roar and a rooster tail of dust spiraled up from the direction of Deerpath Ranch.

Is that what the stallion had heard?

At the center of the sandy plume she saw Mrs. Allen's tangerine-colored truck, going faster than ever.

Chapter Two ❧

"Iknew it was a bad idea. I just knew it," Mrs. Allen said. She slid down from her truck and left the door hanging open. She still wore her artist's smock over her clothes and the Boston bulls weren't with her. "Samantha, when you're old enough to drive, don't. It's a trap, an awful trap that only looks like freedom."

Sam almost laughed. Being warned about the dangers of driving by Mrs. Allen would have been funny, except for her expression. Beyond her jet-black hair and silver jewelry, Mrs. Allen looked sorrowful and shocked.

"Is something wrong?" Sam asked. She felt cold all over. Was it Gram? Dad? She thought of her mom, who had died in a tragic car accident when Sam was little.

Mrs. Allen's hands trembled as she passed them over her face.

"I'm probably overreacting. I dearly hope so, and I won't know anything for a few hours. That's why I came to get you now. You can ride your horse on home while I sit by the telephone." Mrs. Allen took a deep breath. "And wait."

It couldn't be someone in Sam's family, or Mrs. Allen would have said so.

Trying not to be pushy, Sam didn't ask for details. Using two fingers, she picked up the dirty paintbrush, but Mrs. Allen waved her to put it down.

"Leave it. Leave everything and let's go."

Sam did as she was told.

Even though she hurried, Mrs. Allen moved faster. Sam had barely buckled her seat belt when Mrs. Allen put the truck into gear.

For once, she drove slowly, easing over ruts and rocks instead of hitting them.

Finally, Sam had to ask. "Has someone been hurt?"

Mrs. Allen nodded. "My grandson Gabriel."

Sam felt ashamed of her reaction. She flopped against the seat back, weakened by relief that it wasn't someone she loved.

But Mrs. Allen's grandson would be young. Maybe close to her own age.

According to Gram, when Mrs. Allen was a young mother, she'd been obsessed with her art. Although she'd loved her friends and children, her painting had come first. Since her husband's death, that had changed. Mrs. Allen still painted, but she had rebuilt her relationships with her children and grandchildren.

Sam searched for the right thing to say, but her mind was empty.

"I'm only just getting to know him." Mrs. Allen said. Her voice cracked and Sam heard the regret in her words. "He wanted to come stay with me and learn to ride. I put him off, hoping the place would look nicer a couple weeks from now."

Sam thought of all the gardening Mrs. Allen had been doing, and the fence painting.

"I'm sorry," Sam said. It was the truth, and the only thing she could think of to say.

"He and two friends left on a road trip over the weekend. All three had brand new driver's licenses. I could have told them—" Her voice broke and she shook her head. "They wouldn't have listened, I suppose. You see, there was an accident and Gabe—"

Sam spotted a jackrabbit bounding across the road at the same time Mrs. Allen did. Mrs. Allen braked to a complete stop, though the rabbit had already crossed the pavement and disappeared into the brush.

"Gabe's a soccer player," Mrs. Allen said as she

stared after the rabbit. "He made the varsity team as a ninth grader. That's very unusual, but then, he . . ."

Was he dead? A tiny voice in Sam's mind asked the awful question, but she'd never ask it out loud.

"He was conscious, when they brought him into the Denver hospital," Mrs. Allen said, "but he couldn't move his legs."

"I'm so sorry," Sam repeated, but her hands curled into fists of frustration.

She wanted to help, to do *something*. But what? Frozen with the awfulness of this, she thought of her own accident. She could have snapped her spine instead of fracturing her skull. And Jake had been crushed by a falling horse and only broken his leg. They'd both been lucky.

As they drove on, and the pointed roofline of Mrs. Allen's lavender house came into view, Sam felt guilty for ever thinking it looked like a witch's house. Now, the KEEP OUT sign was gone, the rose garden flourished, and the only magic that worked here was the love lavished on forgotten horses.

In the saddle horse corral, Ace trotted to the fence, eyes fixed on the truck, though Calico, Ginger, and Judge, Mrs. Allen's horses, merely swished their tails in recognition.

"Please call when you find out how he is, okay?" Sam asked, before they climbed out of the truck. "And, Mrs. Allen, I don't know what I can do to help, but—"

"Thanks, Sam." Mrs. Allen said it in a dismissing way, like you would to a little kid.

"No, really," Sam insisted. "I'm the one who got you into all this." Sam gestured toward the wide fields that pastured the captive mustangs, then laid her hand on the older woman's arm.

As she looked down at Sam's hand, Mrs. Allen's lip trembled.

"If you think of something, will you please ask me?" Sam added.

"I will," Mrs. Allen promised. "Thank you, Samantha."

This time, she sounded as if she meant it.

Ace took the bit as if he was eager to go home. As Sam folded her horse's silky ears into the headstall on the split ear bridle, she reminded herself there was no need to hurry. She had plenty of time to get home. Besides, in this heat, it wouldn't be smart to push Ace out of a jog, no matter how willing he was to run.

At least it was dry heat, Sam thought as she swung into the saddle. According to Dad, the humidity that came just before a storm was harder on horses.

"No humidity here," Sam told Ace as they jogged away from Deerpath Ranch. "But there's a hot springs over there somewhere, past the old tree house. I'll take you there sometime, good boy."

Ace's ears flicked back to catch her words, but he kept trotting, as if he wanted to get past this part of the trip. The gait wasn't his usual gentle jog; it was more stiff-legged and watchful.

Horse-high weeds stood on each side of the lane, and though Mrs. Allen had cleaned up a lot of her ranch, she'd missed this part. Yellow-white and dry, they didn't move, because there was no wind.

"I don't blame you," Sam told Ace. "You can't see through them."

Maybe the Phantom was still around, Sam thought suddenly. She stood in her stirrups, trying to see past the weeds, but nothing was there.

Sam was about to let Ace lope for just a few yards, when a cicada chirped on her right. Ace shied and Sam snugged her reins. She couldn't reward him by letting him lope now.

As soon as they crossed the highway and the bridge over the La Charla River, Ace relaxed. They were home.

The minute she opened the screen door and entered the kitchen, Sam told Gram about Mrs. Allen's grandson. Frowning, with one hand covering her lips, Gram listened. Twice, she looked toward the phone, but made no move to dial.

"If she's waiting for her daughter to phone," Gram said, "I suppose my call can wait. It's a terrible, helpless feeling not to be able to help a child you love."

Gram kissed Sam's cheek, then waved her hand in front of her nose.

"Gracious, Samantha. You smell like a horse. Why don't you hustle upstairs, then shower and change?"

"Do I have time?" Sam asked. "The hens—"

"I'll be glad to go see if we have eggs," Gram said. "Better that than be cooped up in the car with all that horsehair."

"I can take a hint," Sam said.

When she came back downstairs, not only had Sam showered, she'd washed her hair and blow-dried it, and put on the outfit Gram had given her for her birthday, a short white skirt with matching sandals and a bright emerald-green shirt.

She hadn't been able to get all the paint off her knuckles, but no one would notice.

"You look nice, honey," Dad said as Sam came into the kitchen.

"You, too," Sam answered, but now she knew something was going on.

Dad wore tan slacks. Not jeans. The only time she could remember seeing him in pants other than jeans had been at his wedding to Brynna.

"Dad, is this a celebration, or . . . ?"

He stared at the kitchen clock as if he hadn't heard, then talked over her.

"'Bout time," Dad said, then took Gram's Buick keys from the hook by the kitchen door. "I'll drive."

* * *

When they arrived in Alkali, Brynna's BLM truck was already parked outside Clara's coffee shop.

As the bell on Clara's front door clanged Sam's passage into the aromas of hamburgers, French fries, and upside-down cake, she was more curious than hungry.

Brynna sat at one of Clara's tables with a glass of ice water. She'd changed from her khaki uniform into a summer dress the color of peach ice cream. She was chewing her thumbnail.

"Hi!" Brynna bolted straight up from her seat as she spotted them.

Sam felt as if she were walking underwater as she approached the table. Something was about to happen, but what? Once they sat down, Clara came to their table with her order pad. Sam heard Dad order a fried shrimp dinner. Gram said she'd have the same, plus a pitcher of lemonade for them all to share. Then Brynna ordered soup and crackers.

In July, you didn't eat soup and crackers unless you were sick.

Sam met Clara's eyes and saw she was thinking the same thing. Then a slow smile claimed the old waitress's lips.

"Sam?" Clara asked.

"Uh, how about the chef salad?"

"Good choice," Clara said. Then, raising a hand

toward her own face, she added, "Looks like you've been working outside. You've got some color in your cheeks."

"She's painting fence for Trudy Allen," Dad said.

Sam's confused thoughts made way for surprise as she heard the pride in Dad's voice.

"Good for you," Clara said. She gave a congratulatory nod, then slipped her pencil behind one ear. "I'll be right back with that pitcher of lemonade."

In the silence that followed Clara's departure, Gram's eyes met Dad's across the table.

Now I'll find out what's going on, Sam thought, but suddenly she wondered if they'd brought her to dinner in public to tell her something that would have made her shout if she were at home. What if they thought her manners were too good to do that here? Did they think she would have calmed down by the time they arrived back at River Bend?

"Sam," Dad began.

But suddenly, Sam didn't want to hear what he was about to say.

"So, how are the horses doing in this heat?" Sam swiveled away from Dad to face Brynna.

Brynna knew Sam was talking about the mustangs at Willow Springs Wild Horse Center. "Fine. They're doing just what they would in the wild. Resting up in what shade they can find during the hot part of the day. In fact, I'm glad all over again that we put the weanlings in the pen near the hay storage shelter."

Sam pictured the wall of hay bales, higher than a house. It would cast a block of shade big enough to cool several corrals.

"They're more active at night and early morning, though," Brynna said, then sighed. "And we've been having some fights. Dr. Scott's been treating kicks and bites every day."

"They're too crowded," Sam suggested.

"Way too crowded," Brynna confirmed. "I'll be glad when our adoption auction has come and gone. Then, they'll have more room to move around."

Sam nodded. Although wild horses traveled in family herds, often dozing shoulder-to-shoulder or standing head-to-tail to whisk away flies plaguing each other, the desire to be close could vanish once they were confined with mustang strangers.

Many of the foals born to captive mares had been weaned and were ready to leave their mothers. Since most adopters wanted young horses because they believed they'd be easier to gentle, Brynna had scheduled an auction day for early August.

"Sam," Dad's voice cut across Sam's thoughts, "Brynna and I have something to tell you."

"Okay," she said, in surrender.

Dad gave a quick glance around the coffee shop to see if anyone at other tables was eavesdropping. They weren't, and Clara was busy, scooping ice into a glass pitcher.

" 'Bout the beginning of next year, you're going to

have a new little sister or brother."

What?

Sam's mind spun. She turned toward Brynna again. This time, her stepmother was blushing.

"You're going to have a baby?" Sam asked.

"Yes," Brynna nodded, blue eyes searching Sam's, as if to silently ask how she felt.

How *did* she feel?

Sam tried to do an assessment like you would with someone who'd fallen off a horse. No bleeding, no broken bones, no obvious injuries. But her head seemed to wobble, dizzy with the strangeness of a new member coming into her family.

Gram grinned, clearly delighted, without a trace of surprise. As usual, Sam thought, she'd been the last to learn this secret.

Sam sighed in frustration and told herself she just felt left out. To feel jealous would be ridiculous.

Three sets of eyes watched, waiting for her reaction.

"Wow," she said, and all three of them burst into laughter.

Sam joined in. Then, Clara arrived with the pitcher of lemonade, ice cubes tinkling as she poured.

Silently, Sam hoped, *Please don't let them do something silly like propose a toast.*

She needed a chance to get used to this, before she told the world. Jen might understand, since she'd spent her life as an only child. Jake wouldn't. As the youngest of six brothers, he'd always shared everything. He'd laugh at her shock.

Besides, he was the baby of his family. He wouldn't know how it felt to have a new rival for—

Sam slammed a mental door on that thought and jerked her chin up in stubborn determination.

Dad would always like her best. And so would Gram.

"The beginning of next year?" Sam asked.

"The doctor says January seventeenth," Brynna told her. "But I've done some reading. That date can be very approximate, especially with first babies."

Trust Brynna to research this like the biologist she was.

Sam smiled. Brynna would learn every fact she could in preparation for such an event. Not Gram, though.

Gram leaned both arms on the table. "You'll love being a big sister, Sam, even though it's a lot of work. . . ."

Work? Wait just a minute. This hadn't been her decision. Why was Gram mentioning "big sister" and "work" in the same sentence?

"—worth every second when you hold that soft, sweet-smelling bundle—"

Oh, right. From what she'd heard of diapers, "sweet-smelling" did not describe a baby's aroma.

"—in your arms and they look up into your face with utter trust."

Gram looked like she might cry.

Dad's mouth was set in a stubborn smile, but his eyes searched Sam's, like Brynna's had.

Sam knew she didn't have to worry about Dad asking her to lay her feelings out for everyone to examine. Dad was a cowboy. Cowboys did what had to be done, no matter how they felt about it. He seemed to feel happy. Whether she was happy or not, he'd expect her to process this announcement, and accept it.

I can do that, Sam thought. She gave Dad a nod as Clara arrived, juggling the hot platters while Millie followed with Sam's salad and a cracker basket.

The baby conversation was edged aside by eating. Then, Brynna brought up the BLM's efforts to publicize the mustang auction online, and Sam was struck by an awful thought.

"After the baby's born, you won't stop working at Willow Springs, will you?" Sam asked.

In northern Nevada, Brynna was the best protector the wild horses had within the Bureau of Land Management. She wouldn't desert them for a baby, would she?

"I plan to go back, Sam," Brynna said, but there was something qualified and careful in her voice.

"You have to," Sam insisted. "You're the only one who really understands what the horses need."

"Thanks, Sam, that's sweet."

Not sweet, Sam thought, panicked. It was a fact that made the difference between life and death for the mustangs.

Sam took a long drink of lemonade. She pulled the glass away when she felt the urge to grit her teeth on it.

Norman White had been the BLM official determined to destroy the horses Mrs. Allen had adopted. Twice, he'd taken over at Willow Springs when Brynna traveled.

Norman White thought of the horses as useless animals. No, even that wasn't true. For him, the horses represented numbers. In his equation, mustangs equaled an unneeded expense for the federal government. Taxpayers shouldn't waste money on saving wild horses.

"Oh my gosh, if Mr. White came back —"

"He won't," Brynna said. She broke a cracker in half with a satisfied snap. "He's been promoted."

"Figures," Dad grumbled.

"He's working full time in D.C. now, Sam. That means he won't be in charge of Willow Springs. At least not directly."

"That's all well and good, for now," Dad said, slicing off a bite of his fried shrimp. "But if they've moved him up the line, he'll be makin' decisions. Then you'll have to abide by them and so will we." Dad nodded at Gram and Sam. "And Norman White doesn't know or care what it means to be a rancher fightin' to make a livin'."

"In fairness, that's not what they pay him for," Gram said. "He's not particularly interested. And I guess he doesn't see the value in letting wild horses run the range." Gram sighed and looked down at her plate. "I guess some folks can't appreciate anything without checking its price tag."

"We need a troop of women like Trudy Allen in Washington," Brynna said, picking up her soup spoon for the first time.

Remembering Mrs. Allen's battle with Norman White, Sam stabbed a piece of cheddar cheese in her salad, then a piece of ham, and ate them both. Norman White hadn't stood a chance. The wild horses couldn't have a better advocate.

But that was another subject. Right now, she wanted Brynna's promise to stay at Willow Springs where she could protect the mustangs.

Just then, the door to Clara's jangled open.

"Why, Trudy," Gram said, rising to her feet.

Dad pushed back from the table to stand as Mrs. Allen entered the coffee shop.

Her black skirt blew forward as if she'd been pushed through the door by the hot desert wind that spit sand around her, spattering the linoleum floor.

She struggled to close the screen door against the

wind until Clara came to help. Then Mrs. Allen continued toward them.

"Sit back down, Grace. You, too, Wyatt," Mrs.
Allen said from halfway across the coffee shop. "I
need some help, but you're going to want to think
before you say 'yes.'"

Chapter Three ❧

"What's wrong?" Brynna whispered.

"Her grandson was in a car accident. A bad one," Sam said quickly.

Brynna sucked in a breath. As she exhaled, the breath trembled.

Did Brynna already feel like a mother worrying over her child?

Dad had moved a chair over from another table. Mrs. Allen, her hands steadier than they'd been this afternoon, settled into it.

"Sam will have told you that Gabriel, my daughter Cynthia's boy, was in a car accident." Mrs. Allen barely paused at Gram and Brynna's sympathetic sounds. "It's not as bad as it could be. There's no spinal cord damage."

"Thank God," Brynna said, closing her eyes for an instant.

"At least they don't see any," Mrs. Allen added. "They think it's some sort of bruising, maybe, that's keeping him from moving his legs . . . ?" Mrs. Allen looked at Brynna, Dad, and Gram for their opinions, but they were too troubled to even guess.

"Heavens, I couldn't follow everything I heard. I didn't even talk with Cindy. It was a neighbor of hers that called me back and, I'm humiliated to say I only understood about half of what she told me." Mrs. Allen shook her head. "But that's why I need to be there for my daughter," she added to Sam and Brynna. "Be there for her while she's waiting."

"The waiting is torture," Gram agreed, "and it helps to have a hand to hold."

"Tell us what we can do," Brynna said.

Dad added, "You know you can count on us."

Pride surged through Sam. All four members of her family wanted to help. In a land where help usually meant hard, physical labor, they were no idle offers, either.

"I have a flight out of Reno tomorrow morning. I don't plan to be gone long, a week at most, but I'm hoping that since Sam knows the place, she can take over."

Even though she was startled by the suggestion, Sam realized she wanted to do it. Spending time with

Faith would be great and she wouldn't be away from Tempest long enough for the filly to forget her lessons. Best of all, she'd be right in the midst of the Phantom's territory.

"Trudy, Sam just turned fourteen years old," Gram said.

"C'mon, Gracey, it only means feeding the horses and dogs." Mrs. Allen's tone reminded Sam that Gram and Mrs. Allen were friends. "Doesn't she do that much at home?"

"Sure," Dad said. "We left her to run the place during the cattle drive."

"She couldn't stay alone," Brynna said thoughtfully. "And didn't you say Jen was tied down this week, Sam?"

Sam nodded.

"Oh." Mrs. Allen's voice seemed to run downhill. "I was counting on the two of them. Well, then." Mrs. Allen stared at the coffee shop clock as if it held a solution.

"Wait, what about Callie?" Brynna said. She raised an eyebrow and looked at Dad.

Sam's excitement soared as Dad nodded.

Although she'd only been around Callie for a few weeks, she counted the quirky girl, who was as nuts over horses as she was, a friend.

Dad and Brynna had been on their honeymoon when she'd gotten to know Callie, but Aunt Sue, who'd stayed with Sam, had given them a full report on the older girl.

"That would be great," Sam said, "But Callie has a job." Sam knew how much she needed it, too. Though Callie was only Jake's age, she lived on her own, supporting herself and the wild mare she'd adopted. "And she's gentling Queen. I don't know if she could leave."

"She drives," Dad pointed out. "No reason she couldn't work durin' the day and stay out with you at night."

"And tell her she can bring her horse," Mrs. Allen said. "There's plenty of room in the saddle horse corral, or she can turn her mare out with the mustangs. She can even borrow my horse trailer if she wants. Heaven knows those old beauties of mine haven't been inside it for a decade. I'm not sure Judge ever has."

Mrs. Allen's tongue moistened her lips, as if she were trying to think of more incentives to lure Sam and Callie to Deerpath Ranch. Before she could, Gram leaned close enough to hug her shoulders.

"Trudy, all that's for us to worry over. Now, what time's that flight of yours?"

"Eight o'clock, which means I've got to leave home in the middle of the night. They want me checked in ninety minutes early. Can you believe that?"

"One of us can drive you in," Dad said.

"No sir," Mrs. Allen snapped back at him. "I'll come and go on my own schedule. Letting Sam help out is more than enough."

"We really don't mind driving you," Gram insisted.

"I know exactly what you're thinking, Grace, and you can stop worrying," Mrs. Allen said as she pushed her chair away from the table and stood. "I'll drive careful. Real careful. I want to be there for my daughter, and this summer I'm getting Gabe up on a horse, no matter what."

Since Gram had baked buttermilk shortcakes and left berries sweetening, they decided to have dessert at home. As she watched Dad climb into the BLM truck with Brynna, leaving Sam to ride with Gram in the Buick, Sam kicked herself for thinking Dad had chosen Brynna over her. How stupid. Still, the thought lingered.

"It's a lot to take in, isn't it?" Gram asked after they'd driven a few miles.

"I'm not that surprised," Sam said. "I guess I should have congratulated them, but Mrs. Allen came in. . . ."

"I'm sure they understood. Besides, this isn't a social occasion. It's a change in your life. They know that."

It wasn't such a bad change, Sam thought. Her spirits perked up as she wondered if the baby would be a boy or a girl.

"We're all proud of you for wanting to help Trudy. After all, no one really asked you if you wanted to."

"I do, though," Sam said. "I just didn't say much because, you know, under the circumstances, it seemed awful to say it would be fun if Callie got to come over."

"You handled it just right, dear," Gram said.

Miles ahead on the dark highway, the red brake lights of Brynna's truck flashed on, then vanished as the truck turned left at the bridge over the La Charla River.

As they drove into the ranch yard, Sam thought she heard loud music, but when she climbed out of Gram's car, she realized Blaze sat near the hitching rail, howling.

"What on earth?" Gram said.

Brynna stood near the Border Collie, talking to him, but he only threw his head back further, showing his white throat and ruff. Brynna rubbed her arms, though it wasn't a bit cold.

"Isn't that the eeriest sound?" she asked as Sam approached.

"He looks okay," Sam said, hesitantly.

"What has gotten into you, dog?" Gram asked, then shook her head. "I've seen him do that when he hears sirens."

"That's what Wyatt said. He went in to phone Luke Ely." Brynna shrugged.

Luke Ely, Jake's dad, was the chief of the volunteer fire department. If an emergency involving sirens had been called in, he'd know all about it. Still, the situation made Sam smile, then laugh.

"I love it that we're all wondering what he means," she said. "In Aunt Sue's neighborhood in San Francisco, someone would just tell him to shut up."

"Well, then, they might miss out on some kind of doggy forecast." Gram's tone was only half joking. "There are lots of stories about animals predicting trouble, especially bad weather. Not that I believe all of them."

Sam did. Sort of. She thought of how Tinkerbell, the draft horse that had lived briefly at the ranch, had acted up just before the earthquake a few months ago.

"How do they do it?" Sam asked.

Blaze stopped howling to take a breath and pace in a circle. Sam tried to rumple his ears, but he dodged away and kept walking.

"I know cattle will go around to the protected side of a hill to graze before it storms," Brynna said. "Do you mean that sort of thing?"

"Yes, and field mice fill in the entrances to their burrows, bees hurry home to their hives when the sky turns cloudy, and stay there if a storm's brewing," Gram added. "Oh, and cats are supposed to pay special attention to cleaning over their ears before a storm."

"That sounds like they're feeling barometric pressure," Brynna mused, but then the screen door creaked open, and everyone looked expectantly at Dad.

"False alarm," he said. "No fire or reason for sirens anyplace between here and Reno. Although Luke agrees the weather's ripe for one." Dad looked thoughtful for a minute, then turned to Sam. "Keep an eye out for fire over at Trudy's. She's got the brush cut well back from the house and that's good, but there's an old burn up there. . . ."

"An old burn," Sam repeated, trying to figure it out. "What does that mean?"

"It's a place where a fire has burned through," Gram said. "Two—or was it three?—summers ago, someone threw a cigarette out of a car passing by on the highway. It started a brush fire that burned from the road, all the way to the foothills."

"It took out all the plants and grasses, but most of it's come back. Especially the cheatgrass. But if another fire should come through, it'd burn fast. It acts like kindling when fire reaches it," Dad said. "First thing to do when there's a fire is get the cattle out of those little gullies. . . ."

Sam pictured the gullies and ravines off the path leading up to the Phantom's secret valley. The mustangs grazed in them because they were hidden. But they were also steep-sided and green at the bottom. Could that grass be fuel for flames?

She missed part of what Dad said, but what she had heard was scary enough.

"If a fire starts on the flat and gets a western wind behind it, it'll race over the range and those canyons will act like chimneys."

Sam thought of Mrs. Allen's pastured mustangs. Would they be trapped by the fences meant to protect them?

"There's a lot of dry yellow grass next to where I've been painting the fence," Sam began. "I think it's cheatgrass."

"Don't worry, Sam," Brynna said, reading her mind. "The horses in the sanctuary will be fine. They're not like people, who hang around and gawk when they see fire. They run, and they've got lots of room to get away."

Sam pictured the rolling pastures that had once held the beef cattle of Deerpath Ranch. Picturing the open space made her relax. There were hundreds of acres in which the horses could hide.

"Can I call Callie?" Sam blurted.

"Go ahead," Dad said. "I guess we can spare you for a couple days."

It took her a while to figure out how to contact Callie.

Although Callie Thorson was only seventeen, she was an emancipated minor. As Sam had learned last Christmas from Aunt Sue, that meant her parents had given her permission to live alone and do as she pleased, when they moved away.

Callie had taken a high school equivalency test and graduated early from Darton High. Then, she'd earned a scholarship and work-study job at a Darton beauty college. Although Callie—whose real first name was Calliope—was different from most northern Nevadans with her pierced nose, ever-changing hair color, and interest in the supernatural—she was the sort of hard worker ranch folks admired.

Word got around if you were lazy or didn't pay your bills. Sam remembered Callie explaining that she'd saved most of a cash gift from her grandmother. By scrimping on her own meals and buying a Jeep that had been stuck nose-down in a ditch during a flash flood instead of the new car her grandmother had hoped she'd buy, Callie had saved enough money to adopt Queen.

The beautiful red dun mustang had been the Phantom's lead mare until a split hoof had forced BLM to take her off the range. Callie had even managed to get Queen the corrective shoeing she needed, by bartering her beautician's skills with the farrier's wife.

Sam paged through the telephone book, but found no listing for Callie Thorson.

Next, she tried dialing the phone number for information, but that was a dead end, too.

"Do you think it's possible," Sam asked Gram and

Brynna, "that Callie doesn't have a phone?"

"When you're living on your own and paying your own bills," Brynna said, "it's amazing what you can do without."

"She said she was living on noodles and oranges while she was saving money to adopt Queen," Sam recalled.

"Oh my goodness. We can't have that," Gram said, and Sam could almost see Gram was dreaming up nutritious casseroles. "Let me check what I have in the freezer for you to take to Trudy's place." Gram gave a disapproving tsk of her tongue. "She likes those convenience foods."

"I know," Sam said. She'd eaten her share of TV dinners and frozen pizza at Deerpath Ranch while she was helping Mrs. Allen with Faith.

"You might try calling Callie's parents," Brynna suggested.

Sam knew Callie's parents had moved out of the area to open a new store, but she didn't remember where. She told Brynna, then added, "I think Callie said she was living in someone's garage, but it had been converted into an apartment."

"And they have room for her horse? Oh, I bet she's living with the Monroes." Gram began digging in a drawer for the church phone directory. One minute later she was dialing. A minute after that, Gram wore a satisfied smile as she handed Sam the phone.

"They're calling Callie to the phone," Gram told her.

Waiting, Sam realized she didn't feel a bit awkward about talking with Callie, even though she hadn't talked with her for two months. Then, Callie had called because she'd learned, to her disappointment, that Queen wasn't in foal to Phantom, after all. Before that, Callie had answered Sam's plea for a school fund-raiser to benefit the winterbound mustangs.

"Hello?"

"Hi, Callie? This is Sam For—"

"Sam, I recognize your voice," Callie said. "What's up?"

"Well, I'm really calling for Queen," Sam joked, "but since you answered the phone, you can ask her."

"Stop teasing," Callie ordered. "It's the middle of summer and I haven't done anything but work. I've been saving up my days off and covering for everyone at the beauty college because I've had nothing fun to do. At this rate, I'll be able to take a month off to go snowboarding!"

"Great!" Sam cheered. "How would Queen like to visit some of her long-lost cousins?"

Chapter Four ❧

At seven o'clock the next morning, Sam slung her duffel bag into the pickup truck between herself and Dallas. The bag held everything from summer clothes and wet weather boots to books and her camera.

The truck splashed through a few puddles, but the morning was already hot. Fog simmered up from the wet asphalt as Dallas drove down the highway, toward Deerpath Ranch and Blind Faith Mustang Sanctuary.

"Thought you and that filly'd never stop sayin' good-bye," Dallas teased.

The gray-haired ranch foreman smiled, but kept his eyes on the road.

Sam and Tempest had enjoyed a long nuzzle before parting, but Sam couldn't help it. Since she'd been training Tempest to lead, the rowdy foal had acted like a pet. Sam could hug Tempest's black satin neck and kiss her velvety nose now.

"I haven't been away from her much since she was born," Sam added, "and she's just so sweet."

At a loud thump, Sam glanced back at the horse trailer hooked on behind.

"I hope Ace wasn't jealous," Sam said. Ace didn't act envious of Tempest, but sometimes he surprised her.

"Havin' her mama settle down has helped," Dallas admitted.

Dark Sunshine hadn't acted up since the day at the riverside when she'd chosen Tempest over the Phantom.

"Brynna said that might happen," Sam said. "She said lots of adopted mustangs develop a sense of home wherever they foal."

Dallas gave a skeptical grunt. "We'll see if that young one's sweetness lasts after she's weaned."

Sam didn't ask the foreman why he was always so negative, but when she crossed her arms, he must have guessed what she was thinking.

"I don't want you disappointed, is all," he said. "That filly has the bloodlines to be kinda unruly."

Sam had to agree. With mustang parents like the Phantom and Dark Sunshine, Tempest's sweetness could be temporary.

* * *

Sam twisted in her seat, peering back at Ace in the trailer.

"Almost there," she called to him as they pulled into Deerpath Ranch.

Dallas shook his head, smiling, but Sam wondered if the ranch felt as deserted to him as it did to her.

Sam climbed out of the truck and scanned the ranch for another vehicle. Callie had planned to drive over early in her Jeep, hook up Mrs. Allen's horse trailer, and go back for Queen. But she hadn't arrived yet.

Calico, Ginger, and Judge neighed greetings to Ace as he stamped inside the trailer, but the captive mustangs, roaming far out in their pasture, remained silent.

Dallas eased out of the truck and slammed the door. He stood listening, too.

"I hear them little dogs," he said.

Sam nodded.

Mrs. Allen had said Angel and Imp were used to being inside the house, and well-behaved, so she'd leave them there when she left for the airport.

"I guess I should go tell them 'hi,'" Sam said.

The iron gate barring the path through the garden to the house still had spear-shaped uprights. Pointed and sharp, they looked as dangerous to Sam now as they had when she was a little kid and believed Mrs. Allen was a witch.

The gate opened with a clang. After last night's brief rain, the garden smelled more fragrant than usual. Raindrops trembled on crimson roses growing on one side of the path. On the other side, orange tiger lilies had begun to open and bees flew over them, scouting for pollen.

Even the damp dirt smelled good, Sam noted as she approached the porch steps.

Dallas's boots shuffled behind her and, just before Sam started up the steps, she noticed a rosy-petaled plant Mrs. Allen called mock peach. Hanging amid its branches, a tiny spider's web looked like it had been touched with diamonds. A plain brown spider sat at one edge.

"You see those short little threads she's spun?" Dallas asked, pointing at the web. "That's because it's gonna rain some more. Short threads don't get all weighted down and break like the long ones."

"How did she get so smart?" Sam asked, but Dallas just shook his head. "Or is that just superstition?"

Dallas looked up at a cloud-streaked blue sky. "Guess we'll find out."

Imp and Angel yapped from the other side of the heavy wooden door.

"I got no desire to follow you in, 'less you want me to," Dallas said.

"I'll just check on them and come back." Sam slowly opened the unlocked door.

"Take your time," Dallas said as she slipped inside.

The house was dim, its heavy drapes pulled against the July sunlight. It smelled like coffee and flowers. Sam's gaze fell on a green pottery bowl of roses. It sat on a round table draped with a shawl near the brass phone.

Then she didn't notice anything more, because Imp and Angel took turns springing off the floor, tapping her jeans with their claws.

Their yapping sounded gruff. Had they always sounded like that, or had they barked themselves hoarse since Mrs. Allen left?

"Hush, you two. You're better than a burglar alarm, that's for sure."

Sam spotted a yellow box of dog cookies on the counter next to Mrs. Allen's microwave oven.

She scooped out a handful of the tiny cookies and sprinkled them on the floor, to keep the dogs busy.

"I'll be back," she told them, but they probably couldn't hear her over their crunching.

As Sam came blinking back into daylight, she noticed three things.

First, she saw a cloud had drifted over the sun. Though it was still hot, the bees in the garden had vanished. And Callie had arrived bearing grocery sacks and a canvas suitcase covered with concert stickers. A silver flute was tucked under her arm.

Dallas hadn't offered to take anything from her,

yet. He must have been dazzled by her fuchsia hair.

Staring with cowboy openness, Dallas shook Callie's hand and said, "It was yellow last time, if I'm not mistaken."

"And lime green in between," Callie said.

Her gray eyes sparkled behind wire-framed glasses and a gold stud glittered in her nose.

Joining Dallas's scrutiny, she shifted her armload of stuff and reached up to separate a lock of her own hair from the rest. She held it out in front of one eye. "This started out to be red, white, and blue, for the Fourth of July, but it looked too crazy, even for me."

"I can see how that might be so," Dallas said. "Here, let me tote some of that for you," he added, finally noticing her full arms.

As Callie put everything down, she spotted Sam.

"Sam!" Callie's arms reached wide for a hug, and Sam was enfolded by silky sleeves and musky perfume. "I thought I'd beat you here. I just wanted to drop off my stuff, hook up the trailer, then hurry back for Queen. I know you're eager to see her."

"I really am," Sam said. "It's been since Christmas. I bet she's changed."

"When I look at pictures from that first week, I can really tell a difference," Callie agreed. "She's softer around the eyes and mouth, probably because she's not in pain from that cracked hoof anymore. And I think she's more at peace."

At that, Dallas snorted in disbelief, but instead of arguing, Callie smiled. "Dallas agreed to help me hook up the trailer," she said.

"Not because she offered t'cut my hair," he said, tugging his hat lower on his brow. "Though it was a kind offer."

"Let me take this," Sam said, reaching for Callie's suitcase and a brown paper bag. "And this—oof! What have you got in here?"

The bag was really heavy.

Callie's eyes looked dreamy behind her glasses. "Cantaloupe," she said, "and a big tub of vanilla yogurt. My favorite breakfast."

Dallas recoiled. Sam was pretty sure the most exotic things he'd ever had for breakfast were the fried apple rings Gram had served one Sunday near Thanksgiving, and he'd sniffed suspiciously at those.

"Are you sure you can get it?" Callie said as she fished her Jeep keys from a pocket.

"Yeah, the weight just surprised me. I'll put the bag in the kitchen and your suitcase in the downstairs guest room. It has twin beds."

"Cool," Callie said. "The flute can go on my bed, too, if you don't mind." Then she fidgeted with her keys. "I hate to leave you already."

"Wait, do you think I invited *you* over here? I just wanted to see Queen. Go get her." Sam used her head to gesture toward the Jeep as Callie laughed. "If you don't see me when you get back, I'll be out painting the fence."

It only took Sam a few minutes to arrange Callie's stuff in the room they'd share. Next, she hurried out to check the mangers for Ginger, Judge, and Calico. She found Dallas had not only been there ahead of her, he'd already backed Ace out of the trailer.

Sam imagined new responsibilities settling on her shoulders as she waved good-bye to Dallas and watched him drive away.

"We can do this," she told Ace, then swung into the saddle and rode out to the spot she'd left off painting yesterday.

She finished off one can of paint and was ready to move onto the next can, but it wasn't easy.

She tried to use the stir stick Mrs. Allen had given her to pop the top off the next can, but it didn't work. Even when she tried to lever it off with the blade of the pocket knife she carried in her saddlebag, the lid stayed stuck.

"Saving money doesn't always save time," Sam told Ace where he grazed, ground-tied. His ears flicked in her direction, but he didn't seem to have an opinion.

According to Mrs. Allen, the redwood-colored paint had been in her storage shed for at least ten years, probably longer. When Sam had noticed it was lead-based paint and asked if it was dangerous, Mrs. Allen had made a go-on gesture.

"Sure, it's illegal now, but we're not painting a baby's cradle, Samantha."

"But what if one of the horses cribs?" Sam asked.

"Mustangs don't do that," Mrs. Allen insisted.

Right after Tempest had been born, the vet had noticed bare spots of wood in Dark Sunshine's stall and pointed out that she had been cribbing, due to stress.

"At any rate, people used lead-based paint for a hundred years and you didn't see horses and cows droppin' down dead." Mrs. Allen had stood with her hands perched on the hips of her black skirt, staring at Sam, until she'd given up the argument and started painting.

But now, Sam couldn't get the old lids off.

Because her fingertips felt flat from working to loosen the lids, Sam stood shaking them and staring off toward the Calico Mountains. She didn't see the Phantom or any member of his herd, but she was pretty sure she saw the old burn Dad had mentioned.

While much of the nearby terrain was covered with sagebrush, a swathe of land with a single pine tree in its center looked smooth and green. It was carpeted with cheatgrass and Ace was making a meal of it.

"These cans are like, fossilized," Sam told Ace. This time he just swished his tail and kept grazing.

Frustrated because her day had just begun and

she was already thwarted, Sam set her jaw, jammed her pocket knife blade under another lid, and leaned down with all her weight. She knew she could break her pocket knife, but she was sure the lid would budge first.

"I . . . will . . ."

Had it moved?

". . . get . . ."

Was it coming loose?

". . . this stupid thing . . ."

With a pop and a creak, the lid flipped off, just missing Sam's nose.

"Ha!" she celebrated. "I got it."

Sam painted, trying to finish three sections of the fence before she took a water break. She glanced up when thunder grumbled in some far-off part of the sky, and the hair on her arms stood up with static. She kept painting as the temperature climbed.

She'd forgotten her watch at River Bend Ranch, but Sam figured she'd been working for at least two hours when the crunch of tires turning onto gravel made her look up to see Callie driving slowly into sight with the trailer and Queen.

It must be nearly lunchtime. She deserved a break. Besides, she couldn't wait to see the mare.

Sam tapped the lid back on the paint can, caught Ace's reins, and swung into the saddle. He groaned, unwilling to jog with a full belly, but his long-reaching walk got them to the ranch just as Callie was backing her horse from the trailer.

Slim as a Thoroughbred, with barred legs, a stripe on her spine, and a coat the color of cinnamon, the mare tilted her black-edged ears toward Sam and Ace.

"She's sizing you up," Callie said.

Sam agreed. The red dun mare looked every inch a mustang queen. She'd been a worthy partner for the Phantom.

"She hasn't forgotten she was the lead mare," Sam said.

"It'll be interesting to see how she does out there," Callie said, nodding toward the huge pasture where the adopted mustangs roamed.

"Are you sure you want to turn her out? I thought she'd probably stay in the saddle horse pen. That's where I'm putting Ace."

"That's what I'd do if I could ride her, but I can't," Callie said. "So I might as well let her have some fun."

Sam drew a breath. She admired Callie's faith in her relationship with Queen, but could Callie catch the mare after freedom's energy had surged through her legs once more? Would the other mustangs welcome her? Or would they shun her as an intruder?

Sam smoothed her hand over Ace's shoulder as her eyes strayed to the bite scars on his hindquarters. For a long time, Ace had been the lowest member of the saddle horse herd and he'd paid with strips of hide and hungry nights.

"I don't know anything about the herd hierarchy, except that Roman thinks he's the boss," Sam hinted.

"She'll hold her own." Callie rubbed her cheek against Queen's neck and the haughty mare leaned closer.

Since last winter, Callie and Queen had definitely formed a bond, Sam thought. The mare was an adult—probably a four-year-old, at least—and had never known human companionship, so their friendship was amazing. It just showed what could be created out of patience, love, and curiosity.

"Let me tie Ace, and we'll turn her out," Sam said.

As she led Ace toward Mrs. Allen's barn, Sam heard Angel and Imp barking inside the house.

"Poor little dogs," she mumbled to Ace. They wanted to come out and see what was going on. "They'll have to wait until Queen's out in the pasture, though."

Ace glanced over his shoulder at the mustang mare and gave a snort that said he agreed that Queen wouldn't tolerate the yapping uproar of little dogs.

Sam hurried. She loosened the saddle cinch, removed Ace's headstall, and replaced it with the halter she'd brought from home. Next, she tied him outside Mrs. Allen's barn.

"Sorry, boy, but you're not done for the day," she told him when his head swung around with a look of reproach. "We've got to go back out there and keep painting."

Sam opened the gate into the sanctuary pasture so Callie could lead Queen through. The red dun mare nodded her head right, then left. She stood straight, breathing in the scents of everything around her.

Awareness rippled through Queen as she spotted figures so far out in the pasture they looked like toys. But when Callie unsnapped her lead rope, the mare didn't bolt off after the other horses. Instead, Queen grazed.

Sam only believed the red dun's lack of interest for a second. Queen's pricked ears and the way she snatched mouthfuls of grass showed she was alert to the other mustangs.

"This is a nice place," Callie said, and sighed as she looked around.

"I'll give you the tour later," Sam said. "But now, I should let Imp and Angel out. It sounds like they're going nuts in there."

As soon as Sam opened the door, the black-and-white dogs bounded out. Their toenails scraped on the porch, then clicked on the garden's stepping stones. Finally, they leaped around the girls' ankles, hopping up to lick any skin they could reach.

"Down, you guys," Sam said.

The dogs stopped for a second. They snuffled through flat-faced nostrils, then turned all their attention to Callie while Sam thought about lunch.

"There's a tree house not far from here. How about if we take our sandwiches out to it? I don't think we'll get rained on," Sam said, looking upward.

Gray clouds spread overhead as evenly as a ceiling. Though the wind had picked up, tension lay on the air. Maybe the bees had been right and a storm was on its way.

"Great idea," Callie said. "When we're done eating, I'll help you paint the fence."

Sam knew she should protest that it was Callie's day off, but she didn't. The work would go faster and be more fun with company.

"That'd be great," Sam said. "I'll go make lunch."

When she came back outside with the brown paper bag that held their picnic and tried to shoo the dogs back inside, Angel and Imp panted with rasping breaths and skittered out of reach.

Their round brown eyes stared beseechingly at Callie.

"Let's bring them," she said, and Sam agreed.

Angel and Imp followed obediently at their heels until they reached the tree house. Then, Callie climbed the ladder to the level deck, and held out her arms. Cradling Imp against her chest, Sam took three steps up the ladder, then passed the dog to Callie. Once Callie set Imp down, he wiggled his stumpy tail and barked, encouraging Angel to come join him.

Sam backed down the ladder, scooped up Angel, and ascended the steps again.

"Piece of cake," Sam said as she passed the second dog to Callie.

From the tree house deck, Callie and Sam had lofty views of Deerpath Ranch and all of Mrs. Allen's lands. Past the highway, the La Charla River flowed. They could make out the edge of the sanctuary pasture where its fence of freshly painted brown-red gave way to faded gray. Beyond that boundary, they could see stacked plateaus leading up to the Calico Mountains.

The girls munched their sandwiches and absorbed the stark beauty of the high desert land.

No bigger than a couple of loaves of bread, Imp and Angel lay between Sam and Callie. The black-and-white dogs refused all scraps and panted nervously, but they didn't want to get down.

"You can see where I'm painting," Sam said, pointing. "From down there, it seems like I've done lots more."

There was something about Callie's accepting tranquility that made Sam add, "I saw the Phantom out there yesterday."

Callie's smile lit her face. "I hope you know how rare that is, having a wild horse come to you like that."

Sam ducked her head in acceptance. "He didn't come right up to me, but we saw each other, and this is definitely part of his territory. Mrs. Allen has paintings of mustangs in her studio. She's done a lot of them over the years."

"Cool," Callie said, still staring toward the mountains.

Sam didn't add that Mrs. Allen's favorite models these days were carnivorous plants. But Sam was pretty sure Callie would be just as accepting of that switch.

One of the things she really liked about the older girl was her tolerance of other people.

Sam had just an instant to notice the warmth of the little dogs pressing close to her thigh. Then they whined and flattened their ears as lightning tore the pearl gray sky.

Sam squinted against the brightness. She winced at the hissing crackle and a smell like gunpowder.

Before either girl could speak, thunder boomed.

"We'd better go inside," Sam managed, but Callie was pointing.

At what? Sam stared, eyes skimming down the wind-fluttered sleeve blowing back from Callie's wrist.

"What's burning?" Callie asked.

"I don't see—"

And then she did. Skinny red arms offered up a crazy, twisting white thread.

That's what it looked like until Sam's brain made sense of what she was seeing.

The red arms were the branches of the single flaming pine tree. It stood in the middle of the swathe of cheatgrass and the twisting white threads around the tree were smoke.

The lightning strike had started a fire.

Suddenly Dad's words slammed through Sam's brain.

"If a fire starts on the flat and gets a western wind behind it, it'll race over the range and those canyons will act like chimneys."

Chapter Five &

"Go, go, go!" Sam shouted, but when Callie hesitated before climbing down from the tree house, Sam went first.

Barely looking behind, Sam stepped down on a ladder rung. A sudden wind, so strong it seemed determined to trip her, swirled around her legs.

"We've got to call the volunteer fire department—"

"Before the fire reaches the sanctuary," Callie finished.

With a flash of guilt, Sam realized she'd been thinking of the Phantom. She'd pictured flames licking through brush-filled gullies and narrow ravines, chasing the mustangs, when there were horses—even Ace!—in danger right here.

Her feet stopped and Sam held her arms up.

"I'll take one of the dogs," she shouted.

"Okay," Callie said, and passed one of the wriggling Boston bull terriers to Sam.

"Angel, sweetie, be still," Sam crooned as the dog's slick fur slipped in her fingers. She managed to clamp the dog against her chest with one hand as she held to the ladder with her other, but when Sam's foot reached downward, Angel decided she'd had enough.

Her small jaws clamped a warning bite on Sam's wrist.

"Hey!" Sam yelled, more surprised than hurt. Her grip must have loosened, because Angel writhed free. Sam grappled for the dog, but Angel was already falling.

She hit the ground with a yelp.

Two rungs above Sam, Callie had Imp pinned between her arm and ribs. She looked back.

"Are you okay?"

"Fine," she said, "But Angel—"

Sam's voice broke off with a cough, but her feet kept moving. She reached the ground in time to see Angel stand, shake the dirt from her coat, and begin barking.

As soon as Callie reached the ground and released Imp, the dogs scampered two laps around the tree, then raced for the house.

Sam and Callie took off after them, but when their shoulders brushed for the second time, Sam realized they were both staring toward the fire.

Orange flames danced amid the smoke. The winds warred for control, blowing both fire and smoke from side to side.

"The horses are penned," Sam gasped, remembering the barn fire at River Bend Ranch. Trapped and forgotten inside the high-sided round pen, Dark Sunshine had screamed to be freed. "Should we let them out?"

"They're safe for now," Callie said. "If the fire truck comes . . ."

Sam nodded and kept running. The firefighters would be busy fighting the blaze. Loose horses would just add to the confusion.

"Just run," Callie shouted.

"I've gotta . . ." Sam bolted toward the barn where Ace rolled his eyes and jerked at his halter rope.

Her knot was holding, but she couldn't leave him tied. Anything could happen.

"Ace, it's okay boy."

The gelding's whinny said he knew very well that nothing was okay.

Sam tugged the loose end of her quick-release knot and ran toward the corral, towing Ace. He followed but his steps veered from side to side, and when she opened the gate and he saw Calico, Ginger, and Judge trotting nervously around their pen, Ace refused to enter.

"Ace!" Sam shouted. "Knock it off!"

Then Sam closed her eyes in frustration. At herself.

Wise from his years on the range, Ace knew the scent of smoke meant danger. He'd learned, too, that when humans acted frantic and out of control, there was trouble.

Callie had run inside to call the fire department. What would it hurt to comfort Ace, just a little?

"Sorry, pretty boy," Sam said. As soon as she let the rope fall loose between them the horse stepped nearer.

Ace turned his head aside, but one eye watched her. His lips moved as if grumbling what he thought of her craziness.

"Just go in with them, Ace," Sam said, but then the wind shifted, bringing smells of heat and smoke. Ace's nostrils widened and closed, and Sam's mind raced ahead. "Maybe in a few minutes I'll ask Callie to give you a ride home."

Head bobbing so that his black forelock covered, then cleared from his eyes and the star on his forehead, Ace followed her into the corral. The two paint mares and the old bay looked nervous, but Sam was pretty sure they weren't terrified.

Then they proved it. As she set Ace loose with a pat on the rump, the other horses rushed to stand guard at their empty feed bins.

Thunder rolled overhead, making Sam walk faster. When lightning crackled, she ran. Rain began

The Wildest Heart **61**

pattering down. But before Sam could feel relieved, she heard more crackling. Not lightning this time, but brush burning. When she looked up, a yellow haze of smoke drifted across the clouds.

The wrought-iron gate clanged as Sam entered the shady garden and saw Callie coming down the concrete path that looped around the side of Mrs. Allen's house. The path led to Mrs. Allen's art studio, a separate building, with high, round windows. Callie carried Imp and Angel.

Sam's mind raced. Callie should have been in the house by now, calling the fire department!

"They were hiding back there," Callie said. "I couldn't leave them on their own."

"I bet they were looking for Mrs. Allen," Sam said. She felt sorry for the little dogs. Callie was right — Imp and Angel weren't smart in the way Ace was. Left on his own, the mustang might survive a fire. Those two little dogs wouldn't stand a chance. But how much closer had the fire burned in five minutes?

There was no time to worry about it.

"I'll do it," Sam said, but Callie was right beside her. "There's a brush truck at Three Ponies Ranch," Sam added, as they nearly fell through the front door together. "It should be able to get here right away."

Grateful she knew where to find the telephone from the time she'd spent here before, Sam turned to the round table draped with what looked like a gypsy shawl.

While Sam dialed, Callie ran fresh water into a bowl for the panting dogs.

Before she'd even finished dialing, Sam heard the faraway wail of a siren.

Someone else must have sighted the smoke and reported it. But Sam didn't hang up. What if lightning had started more than one fire?

It sounded like the truck was coming from Three Ponies Ranch. Relief rushed through her as she thought of Luke Ely, chief of the volunteer fire department, surrounded by his experienced and level-headed sons. Would Luke be home from work? For a minute she couldn't remember which day it was, but then she thought of Bryan and Quinn and Jake. They'd rush to help, even if Luke was away.

"It's still just ringing," Sam told Callie.

Callie gave a half nod. "Wait for the dispatcher, anyway. One truck might not be enough."

Chills, like being wrapped in a wet sheet, made Sam shiver.

Callie was right. If the fire raged out of control, one truck couldn't fight both sides of the blaze. Part of it could race toward wild horse country while the other part swept toward Deerpath Ranch. It wouldn't, would it? Wouldn't the wind push it in one direction?

The phone kept ringing—where? In Darton? At the county offices where she'd met with Sheriff Ballard? Why wasn't someone answering? Sam wondered as she remembered the wind tossing the flames back and forth, warring for control.

"Fire department."

In an instant, all the emergency drills she'd recited in elementary school came back to Sam.

"This is Samantha Forster. I'm at Deerpath Ranch, Mrs. Allen's place?" Sam heard the dispatcher's quiet "go ahead" and maybe the tapping of computer keys. "A lightning strike started a fire out on the . . ." Sam paused, trying to picture a compass. Which side of the ranch was burning? Which direction?

"We've already got a volunteer truck started your way," the dispatcher said. "One of Luke Ely's boys called it in. They're right by you, and the Darton Fire Department's been notified to stand by. They're in radio contact with each other."

Sam met Callie's eyes and gave her an "okay" sign.

"If the volunteers don't think they can knock down the fire on their own, we'll tone out Darton."

Tone out.

Sam wasn't certain what that meant, but she remembered hearing Dad's volunteer fire department radio giving high-pitched sounds, and Gram saying the emergency was for another department.

Whatever. Help was coming.

"Samantha?" the dispatcher said.

"Yes," Sam answered, but she was watching

Callie, thinking she looked awfully pale.

"Ask if we should leave," Callie instructed.

No, Sam thought. She didn't want to ask.

She had to stay. She'd promised Mrs. Allen that she'd take care of the captive mustangs. And she had to ask the firefighters if the flames were burning toward the foothill canyons.

If they were, she had to tell the firefighters about the wild horses. If she didn't stay to do it, who would?

"Should we evacuate?" Callie demanded, raising her voice.

The dispatcher must have heard. "Samantha, are you listening?"

"Yes," Sam said, at last.

"It's always smart to evacuate before you're ordered to, but Chief Ely will be on scene in . . ." The dispatcher paused. Sam heard a squawk and the buzz of radios before the dispatcher continued. "A minute or two. Follow his directions."

"Okay," Sam said and then she hung up.

"The mustangs are probably okay," Callie said.

Which mustangs? Sam's mind ping-ponged between the captive herd, seeing Roman, Belle, Faith, the sorrel with the twisted legs . . . and the Phantom's wild band with the two blood bays, the big honey-colored mare, the bay colt with the white patch over one eye that she called Pirate, and the mighty silver stallion who'd once been hers.

Suddenly, Sam swallowed hard, remembering

Queen. Callie had a horse to worry over, too.

"They've got plenty of room to run away from the fire," Sam said.

"But what about Mrs. Allen's three, and Ace?"

"We have the trailer," Sam reminded her, but a sour taste filled her mouth. They had a two-horse trailer. Was there time to move all four horses?

"Okay." Callie pushed pink bangs away from her wire-rimmed glasses. Sam could see her mind whirling behind her gray eyes. Callie was probably troubled by the same thoughts.

"And I could take the dogs with me," Callie said slowly.

"Good idea," Sam said. "And since River Bend is on the other side of the river, but still close—"

"I'll take them there," Callie finished. "But while I'm doing that," Callie said, shaking her head, "I can't leave you here."

"Don't worry about it," Sam began.

"Don't worry? Are you joking?" Callie came closer to snapping than Sam had ever heard her.

"No, I just—"

"If it's serious enough to evacuate the horses and dogs"—Callie's voice was too level and controlled—"then you have to leave."

"It's just a precaution," Sam insisted.

"Do you really expect me to just desert you here with a fire"—she motioned vaguely—"like, roaring down on you?"

Sam blocked out the image. "Okay, you're allowed to worry, and I promise to talk with Jake's dad as soon as I can."

"And if he says to leave, you'll do it," Callie added, pinning Sam down. "Right?"

"Right," Sam said. Then, she'd bet her smile turned sickly, and not because she was afraid of the fire. Dad and Gram would freak out when they realized she was facing the fire without them.

In fact, since Dad was part of the volunteer fire department, the emergency radio that usually sat in the living room with a red light glowing had probably started beeping and giving orders. Dad might be on his way over right now.

The dogs clicked to the front door and sniffed at the bottom of it. Was the smoke heavier?

The sirens were louder, closer.

Suddenly, heavy footfalls sounded on the walk outside.

Then the pounding of a fist made the wooden door shudder. The little dogs barked in a high-pitched frenzy as a voice boomed, "Let's go! Everybody out!"

Chapter Six ∾

"I'm not leaving," Sam told Callie as the fist hammered at the door, but the older girl must have seen the fear mixed with Sam's stubbornness, because she pretended not to care.

"Suit yourself," Callie shouted over the pounding at the door. "And when you do decide to take off, bring my flute," Callie said. "No way would I put it in the Jeep with Imp and Angel."

"Someone needs to stay and watch the horses," Sam protested.

Her voice was way too loud, as the sirens cut to silence and the pounding stopped.

Sam couldn't prick up her ears like the dogs did, but it sounded as if the truck had stopped farther out than the ranch gates.

Sam was reaching for the doorknob, about to go out and explain she had to stay with the horses, when the front door swung open.

The dogs jumped back.

Outside, smoke hung like fog. Its smell rushed in, overcoming the scent of Mrs. Allen's roses. Standing amid the thick smoke was Jake Ely.

Dressed in bright yellow "turnouts," with his black hair tied back and tucked inside his collar, Jake looked like a real firefighter. Sam wondered why she felt a wave of relief at the sight of him. Especially since she had no intention of doing what he'd shouted through the door.

"I mighta known," Jake said.

Jake's low voice revived Imp and Angel. Yapping and drooling, they lunged toward him.

"Oh, get back," Callie scolded. Then, grabbing Sam's arm, she slipped outside and pulled the door closed behind them, leaving the dogs indoors.

"You need to leave the ranch," Jake said. "They never should have put the propane tank so close to the house."

Sam hadn't noticed the tank of propane Mrs. Allen used as heating fuel. Now, she did. The white tank looked like a small submarine, and it was filled with flammable gas. If the tank got too hot, it would explode.

"I'm outta here," Callie said, though she didn't take a step. "I trust Queen to take care of herself."

Jake looked satisfied as he motioned for the girls to walk ahead of him.

Callie watched Sam.

Sam set her teeth against each other. How could she balance her safety with that of the horses?

This was no time to bicker with Jake, but she said, "The lady at the fire department told me to wait for your dad, since he's the chief."

Jake's eyes widened. Sam could see he was offended, but just for a second.

"C'mon," he said, then strode toward the green fire truck parked outside the ranch gates.

Sam followed, but she only glanced at Luke Ely and the other guys in yellow turnouts clustered around him. They were all staring at the fire, and Sam stopped stone-still as her eyes followed theirs.

Her pulse pounded in her temples, throat, and wrists, and her mouth turned dry.

The fire had quadrupled in size. It had burned just a few yards along the fence line before veering away from the sanctuary pasture. Now it gobbled cheatgrass, leaving a black scorch behind as it swooped toward the foothills.

"Stop it!" Sam shouted, then she turned to Jake. "Can't you please stop the fire?"

For an instant, Jake's eyes showed he was her friend, the guy she'd grown up with.

"It's okay, Brat," he said, in a soothing tone. "It's burnin' away from us."

"I know," she said. "I'm not scared, it's . . ."

Jake's sympathy got all mixed up with her mental images of wild things fleeing hungry flames.

"The animals," Sam said, but while she tried to focus her thoughts, Jake returned to the firefighter's attitude he'd pulled on along with his turnouts.

"Our first responsibility is to protect people and structures," he said.

"But the people and structures are just fine!" Sam cried.

The gray-white fire hoses were rolled out to battle the flames. Jake's brothers, Quinn and Bryan, and a cowboy she didn't recognize, seemed almost lazy as they aimed water spray at the fire.

And Jake's dad was just standing there!

"It's burning away from the house. You just said so," Sam pointed out, when Jake didn't seem to understand. "So there's no reason to evacuate, and you guys can go around there"—she broke off to point at the sheet of flame sweeping toward the hills—"and put it out."

Sam tried to sound patient, but she'd bet she was doing a bad job of it. Even though Callie hung back a few steps, Sam knew she felt frustrated, too. Callie just wasn't arguing because she didn't know Jake as well.

"Can I just talk to your dad?" Sam asked.

"He's busy."

Jake's voice left no room for questions, and Sam saw Luke Ely was speaking into a handheld radio.

He was the chief, Sam reminded herself. He was in touch with the Darton fire department.

Frustration kept swelling inside Sam. Either Jake and the other firefighters were blind, or she was missing something. That had to be it, because they couldn't all be so hard-hearted. Could they?

As if he'd heard, Jake's brother Quinn surrendered his position on the hose to another man.

Skinny and tall, Quinn had a porcupine-sharp crewcut. He looked nothing like Jake as he strode toward them, carrying his helmet by the chin strap. Quinn was on student council at school and he'd helped her pull a trick or two on Jake, but once he reached them, his voice was honey-sweet, as if he were trying to calm her, too.

"Don't worry, you're safe," Quinn said.

"Who cares about *my* safety?" she began.

"You're always safe in the black," Quinn went on, as he pointed. "The first flames burned along the fence line. So even if the wind shifts and the fire comes back this way, you're okay. There's nothing for it to burn in the black."

When Sam waved her hands, he stopped talking, eyebrows raised in surprise. "I'm not worried about getting hurt. The fire is going up the canyon."

Quinn shot a quick glance at his brother, but Jake's expression reminded Sam of a closed door.

"It might burn that far, depending on the winds," Quinn said, squinting toward the hills. "Luckily, there's only cheatgrass between here and there. Really, it's doin' a good job of clearing things out. Lots of ranchers apply for permits and do a controlled burn so that they can plant. Mrs. Allen doesn't have to go to all that trouble."

All at once, Jake and Quinn stiffened, shrugged, and went back to work as their dad approached.

Luke Ely was taller than Dad. His pronounced cheekbones and long jaw made him look like a man who was used to giving orders and having them obeyed. Sam knew Jake's dad had a great smile, but it was hard to picture it. As he came her way, he looked every inch a fire chief.

"It'd be a good idea to get those older horses out of here," he said to Callie. "They suffer from smoke inhalation just like people."

"Got it," Callie said, and her car keys were already in her hand as she left.

"Now, what's up with you?" he asked Sam.

Jake's dad sounded impatient, but faintly amused. Maybe.

"Quinn and Jake were both telling me there's no reason to fight the fire over there," Sam said, pointing. "And, I understand about you having to stay here and protect homes and barns first, but since it's all burned off—"

"It isn't," Luke interrupted. "It's burnin' spotty, because of moisture in the low places."

Sam swallowed hard as he indicated the place

where she'd left the paint cans. She couldn't see them from here, but she could imagine dampness from the passing storm. It probably wouldn't be damp enough, Sam thought, as she heard more crackling.

"There's plenty left to burn if it turns back this way," Luke said. "That's why I left Nate down there with what equipment I could spare, and that's why we're taking a stand here."

The sound of a distressed neigh made Sam turn away from Luke. She squinted back toward the ranch yard. She could make out Callie in the corral and see Ace trotting uneasily around it. She could see only one pinto. Callie must have already loaded the other, but now she was battling Judge. Tossing his black mane, the old gelding reared, huffed, and resisted the pull on the halter rope.

"Samantha." Luke's voice jerked her attention back. "I need you to return to the house and stay there, if you're not leaving with Callie."

"I'm not," she said.

Callie drove past, windows rolled up against the smoke, but Sam could see she was frowning.

Sam didn't wave. She drew a breath, trying to ask more, explain more, but her eyes were fixed on a tower of smoke mingling with the gray clouds. She couldn't tell them apart. Smoke veiled the sun, turning it into a tan disk surrounded by a dull yellow ring. Everywhere the smoke wavered.

Fire didn't have a mind of its own. If it did, she'd

think the flames were trying to decide in which direction to charge next.

"Sam, you're going to have to spit it out," Luke snapped. "I've got duties here."

Sam's fists curled so tightly, her fingernails bit into her palms.

"If the fire keeps burning toward the hills, it'll get into the canyons. My dad says they'll act just like a chimney."

Luke gave a nod, but then a tone from his radio distracted him. After a short sentence, he turned back to her.

"Wyatt's right. That area's a disaster waiting to happen. It hasn't burned off in years, which means there's lots of fuel.

"It looks awful when you see black, charred trees where a fire's gone through, but a fire can be a blessing. Old brush is gone. Big animals can move through areas that have been too dense for them. New seeds get sun for the first time and the ashes act like fertilizer. That's how nature does it and we've been interferin', settin' ourselves up—"

As Luke turned to his radio again, Sam rubbed her arms against a sudden gust of wind, but it wasn't cold. The smoky summer wind might have gusted from an oven.

"We got trouble," Luke Ely shouted toward the nearest firefighters.

Sam moved with the men as they fought for a

better view of the area where Luke had assigned Nate.

She saw wild horses on the run.

Led by a young bay galloping full out, the horses stampeded down from the hills. What could they be running from? Had wind-borne sparks blown and started a fire they couldn't see from here? Was a fire already burning into the canyon?

When the bay tossed his head, showing a patch of white over one eye, Sam recognized Pirate. Just behind him ran the red roan filly she thought of as Sugar. The horses bumped shoulders and faltered. For a second, the filly veered off course as if the smoke stung her eyes. But then she must have heard the golden-brown mare, trying to keep up, because Sugar's roan legs stretched as she pursued Pirate.

The golden-brown horse was the Phantom's lead mare. Usually, she controlled the herd while the silver stallion watched from above, or hung back where he could see his entire band. But where was he now?

While Sam stood transfixed by the horses' hasty and clumsy descent, Jake and Quinn bolted back toward the other firefighters, who were already hefting the hose. It was then that Sam heard the sound of a cyclone, a tornado, some wild storm rushing their way. Only it wasn't a storm; it was a freakish gale created by the fire.

When Sam turned back to look for the Phantom once more, she could barely see the herd. Dark smoke reduced the mustangs to shadows darting and stumbling in the direction of the captive horses.

Sam squinted and used her hand to shade her eyes, as if that could keep them from tearing up from the smoke.

Something moved, far out in the pasture. Did the wild herd think the other horses were running to safety?

That could be it, Sam decided.

Once, Dark Sunshine had been a decoy, luring other horses into a trap. Sometimes BLM loosed a domestic horse just ahead of wild ones as they fled a hovering helicopter, and they followed the "Judas horse" into a camouflaged corral. Maybe the same thing was happening now.

Pirate reached the pasture fence and raced up and down, looking for a way in. From where she stood, Sam thought he was near the gate, where she'd been painting. What if she ran down and let the wild mustangs into the pasture? Once the horses were confined, the firefighters could protect them.

But if she ran down there, the mustangs would flee. She had to make this decision alone. Jake and the other firefighters were busy. Callie was gone.

Only the fire would help her make this decision.

Red flames danced like tightrope walkers along the top rail of the fence, burning closer and closer to Pirate. He circled away from the fence, looking as if he'd backed up to jump.

She'd heard of fear-maddened horses breaking

free of those leading them out of burning barns, to run back to stalls because they were home. But those were domestic horses.

Pirate's determination to run through flames, into the sanctuary pasture, made no sense.

The lead mare wanted to force him back, but clanging metal, the huff from the fire truck's engine, the shouting men, and a dark shroud of smoke turned her trot into a shambles of confusion.

Suddenly a whirlwind of movement swept through the milling herd.

Glinting brightly through the smoke, the Phantom galloped downhill. He ignored the worn path, leaping in sharp turns to make his way through the brush, to take charge of his band.

Chapter Seven ∽

$\mathcal{S}$am didn't know whether she felt relieved or terrified as she watched the stallion rush down with ears so flat they were hidden by his swirling silver mane.

His mares' turbulent shifting turned to calm as the stallion's presence settled them. The honey-colored mare's uncertainty had caused chaos. The Phantom was hurried, but sure.

Sam pictured the stallion's actions.

Brandishing teeth and hooves, he'd push the herd away from here, back to their secret valley, and leave Pirate to tag along.

But he didn't. Instead of turning his band toward the mountains, the Phantom passed through, then lowered his head into a herding posture.

Pirate was probably a yearling, but the Phantom's body language was clear. *Act like a baby and I'll treat you like one.*

The roan filly saw her sire coming and fled. Swiveling on her heels like a cutting horse, she returned to the herd, leaving Pirate to face his father alone.

Pirate was clearly nervous. He saw the Phantom bearing down on him, but the colt didn't run away. He skittered sideways, head swinging to view everything around him, but whatever had drawn him to the pasture kept him there.

Just yards away from Pirate, the Phantom slowed. Sam heard the beat of each hoof. His ears pricked forward, tips trembling as he strained to listen, but his head stayed low, as if the stallion were trying to ignore his misgivings.

But then, he must have known something was terribly wrong.

His front hooves skidded in a dust cloud. His eyes rolled white, but his head was still lifting as two hollow *zip pops* split the air. Like huge fireworks launched into the sky, the paint cans exploded. Blasting like bombs, they detonated right in front of the mustangs.

"No!" Sam screamed.

The horses screamed with her. Thunder rumbled from their hooves and overhead. Through roiling smoke, she saw horses fall. How many? Which ones?

Sam couldn't tell. Smoke stung her eyes and nose. Her chest burned as she ran, trying not to breathe in the thick gray air.

Not the Phantom, oh please.

But he was right there. It had to be him, falling. And Pirate. Their slender, delicate legs had been steps from the exploding cans.

Holding her breath, Sam remembered how firmly she'd tamped down the lids. If they'd exploded off, they'd be like giant, flat bullets.

Another explosion rocked through the air. Then another.

Four cans. That had to be all of them.

Were the horses down and helpless in the blast?

Black timbers rocked apart. Half of the fence sagged toward the earth and the other jutted up like black fingers.

The explosion, or maybe the fire, had destroyed a section of fence and the lead mare saw it as rescue. With bared teeth and slamming shoulders, the big mare herded the mustangs through the opening, away from the flames and smoke and noise, after the other horses, who were no more than silhouettes on the hazy horizon.

Running after them, Sam's whole world bounced around her. Her legs stretched in steps as long-reaching as her hip sockets would allow. Tears from the smoke blurred her vision as she searched for the Phantom. He wasn't with his herd. Even as a smoky shadow she would have recognized him.

"We've got two down. Call the vet!" Luke Ely shouted at someone. Her? Should she run back to the house? Confusion and desperation whirled through Sam, but she couldn't go back. Not until she saw her horse.

Two thoughts eased her mind. If Luke Ely thought the horses needed a vet, they weren't dead. And the firefighters had radios. They could summon Dr. Scott in a fraction of the time it would take her to run back to the house and phone.

Sam ran through a mist from the fire hose. Charred wet brush released a sour stench. Sizzling and steamy, waves of wet, white smoke rushed at her.

The fire that had flared along the fence was out. Finally, Luke must have ordered the volunteers to turn their hoses on the tail of the fire rushing toward the mountains.

Sirens wailed. Huge truck tires hit ruts and chugged on, passing her, but Sam barely noticed the commotion. She only saw Jake, ahead of her. Jake, holding his hands wide apart, palms toward her, warning her back.

It wasn't the stern gesture that frightened her. Far worse was his frown of pity.

"Get out of my way!" Sam shouted, but Jake blocked her.

Beyond Jake, Sam glimpsed Luke, shaking his head "no."

"Sam, stop fighting me."

She tried to run through Jake, to bull past him, but he was too strong.

She had to see. She didn't want to, but desperation swelled within her chest until she felt it, too, would explode.

Jake grabbed her forearms and gave them a shake.

"Listen to me," he said. "Sam, are you listening?"

She couldn't twist loose. She couldn't see past him. So she listened.

"It's him," Jake said, and though she'd wanted to know, the two words ripped like knives. "He's down. He's breathing, though. He's alive."

Jake waited, staring at her until she nodded, before adding, "There's a colt, too, with a white patch."

Sam realized she was nodding over and over again.

Pirate and the Phantom. Both were down. Both were hurt or they wouldn't still be there.

"What wrong with them?"

"Don't know. They're all splattered with red. . . ."

A moan arose and Sam only realized it was hers and that her hands had tried to fly up to cover her ears, to block the awful words, when Jake's grip tightened on her arms.

"Don't think it's blood." Jake was shaking his head. "It doesn't look like blood."

Hope surged through her along with a possibility.

"The paint? Could it be? Because . . ." Sam shook her head as her teeth started chattering. "The p-paint's b-b-brownish red. Redwood. Jake, could it . . . ?"

"Yeah." Jake looked relieved. "That must be why all those little spot fires flared up, too. It splattered, but we got 'em."

Beyond Jake, there was thrashing and a groan of effort.

"Stay back," Luke Ely said.

Sam heard boot soles crunch against the ground. She smelled a charcoal scent stirred by movement.

"Please let me go to him," Sam begged.

"Let 'im be, Sam," Jake told her. "I know you love him, but he's a wild thing. You're only gonna add to his—" Jake broke off, knowing she'd fill in the awful blank.

Pain? Confusion? Terror?

The memory of the mighty stallion in the rodeo arena flashed through Sam's mind. He'd sunk to his knees, then fallen on his side. If that's what lay beyond Jake, she'd hate it, but she could take it.

"Whatever's goin' on in his head, you can't help. If he can get up, he'll get outta here. If he can't, Dr. Scott will be here soon," Jake finished.

She could take it, but her horse might not be comforted.

A shuddering sigh shook Sam. She nodded.

"Okay," she said. "I won't move a step closer. I

promise, Jake. Just please, get out of my way so I can see him."

Jake's fingers loosened, one by one, from her left forearm. Sam looked up into his eyes as he released her right arm, too.

Jake stood with his hands raised for a second. Did he think she'd fall and he'd have to catch her? No, he stepped aside and Sam was almost sorry.

War movies showed scenes like this.

A pale horse spattered with scarlet lay on the blackened earth. Just feet away, another horse, face scorched, thrashed as if fighting to rise, but his eyes were closed, lids fluttering as if he were trapped in a nightmare.

"What's wrong with them?" Sam barely breathed the words.

She and Jake stood about ten feet from the horses, but they'd hear, and she didn't want to frighten them more.

Far away, Sam heard the firefighters congratulating each other. The fire was out. But Jake had heard her. He shook his head, concentrating on the horses.

Sam kept her promise. She moved no closer, but she squatted and stared.

The Phantom's rib cage rose with each breath. Dark-gray streaks marked his glossy hide and dots of paint spotted his head and ears.

From lowering his head when he'd tried to herd Pirate out of danger, she thought.

His head had been right there when the cans exploded from the fire's heat. Now his fine-boned head lay on the blackened ground.

How long ago had the rain stopped? When had the sun emerged from the clouds and smoke? Sam didn't know the answers, but she knew the earth must be hot and the burned weeds must be prickling the delicate skin around the stallion's eyes and lips. She wanted to pillow his head in her lap.

But if he woke, lashing out in panic, he might hurt himself more.

Strands of his mane and tail lifted on the breeze. Otherwise, he didn't move. She ached to do something for him, but what?

A tiny sound made Sam look down. Dark spots showed on the right knee of her jeans. Only then did she realize her face was wet with so many tears, they'd begun dripping off her chin.

With the back of one wrist, Sam wiped her eyes and kept watching.

She didn't know how long the horses lay still. Five minutes? Fifty?

At last, Jake's dad squatted beside her.

"Could be they're just gatherin' strength. Hard to believe, but those cans blowin' all at once caused sort of a concussion. Did you feel it?"

Sam shook her head "no," but Jake had been closer and he nodded.

"Kinda like a shock wave," he said.

Sam tried to think how that would affect horses. An explosion — or a concussion — would be something completely outside their experience. The only thing they could compare it to would be a storm. The thunder of the concussion, the lightning flash of the explosion. They knew how to react to predators, to drought and floods and intruders. They'd even learned to flee cars and motorcycles, but exploding paint cans in the midst of a brush fire?

Some people laughed at horses when they shied at scraps of paper or odd-shaped rocks, but horses judged every unfamiliar thing a threat and it had helped them survive centuries of change.

Thinking like a horse, Sam guessed that explained why the horses had bolted through the opening in the fence. It had been the quickest escape and they saw the others running to safety.

Sighing, Sam forgot all about Jake and his dad. Her world shrank to the few yards of earth around the fallen horses. She was dimly aware of truck tires and voices, but she paid no attention.

She wanted to scoot close enough to whisper the Phantom's secret name. Even in his unconscious state, it might soothe him.

Zanzibar. With tenderness, she thought the name toward the stallion. And hoped.

Sam jumped when a hand touched her shoulder. She looked up to see Dr. Scott. Young and blond, the veterinarian wore black-rimmed glasses. The lenses were grimy with smoke. The first time she'd met him, even though he'd been tending the Phantom's reaction to a drug overdose, Dr. Scott had also worn a hopeful expression. He didn't wear one now.

Behind him, the volunteer firefighters sprayed water on tiny tongues of flame as they flared up here and there. Beyond them, the Darton fire truck prowled the perimeter of the blaze flickering up the mountain.

The storm had moved on, leaving behind destruction and the good, clean smell of storm-hammered sage.

With a strange detachment, Sam wondered if the sky would have dropped the same lightning bolt, even if horses and people had never settled here. Probably so. Nature wasn't out to get them. Storms happened whether living things were helped or hurt by them.

Sam could still see grass all around. It looked as if there was still plenty of graze for the horses. That was good.

It seemed weird to her that there were suddenly so many people around and no one had spoken to her.

Weird, until she realized, with a sickening certainty, that they'd seen her crouched near the mustangs and left her alone to grieve.

But she wasn't grieving! The horses weren't dead.

Any minute they'd stand up, kick their heels, and gallop for home.

As if he'd seen in his mind what she had in hers, the Phantom's eyes opened.

"Hey, boy," Sam whispered.

Even before he raised his head off the ground, the stallion's eyes flashed brown and fierce. They might have been the eyes of an eagle.

His nostrils flared as his muzzle lifted. His head rose away from the ground, crinkling his dappled neck. For an instant, the stallion's eyes met hers and he gave a soft nicker.

He must have felt safe, because once he scrambled to his feet and faced away from her, he didn't bolt. He must be trying to recover from his shock.

Forelegs braced apart, head hanging, the stallion winced. Something hurt. A pulled muscle from his fall, Sam hoped, or a scrape so small she couldn't see it.

But why were his ears twitching forward, then back and forward again, with such crazy energy?

Then the stallion shook his head.

At first Sam thought the Phantom was only sending his forelock out of his eyes, but he shook his head again. Standing behind him as she was, Sam noticed he shook so vigorously, his entire tail swung with the movement.

The stallion's neck curved. His head jerked toward his shoulder. Then his front leg struck out, but it didn't come near his head. Still, his gestures reminded her of Blaze trying to get a foxtail out of his ear.

"Did you see that?" Sam asked the vet.

When he didn't answer, she glanced at Dr. Scott. His fingertip pressed against the nosepiece of his glasses and he gave a curt nod.

"What's he doing?" she asked.

The stallion snorted. This time he shook his head so hard his ears made a faint flutter.

"He could have something in his ears," Dr. Scott suggested. "Debris from the explosion."

The vet didn't sound convinced, and Sam found herself snatching looks at him, trying to read his expression, while she watched the Phantom.

When the stallion's gaze shifted to the pasture and he uttered a longing neigh, Dr. Scott slammed his hands together in a loud clap.

Sam jumped, touching her chest at the sudden stampeding of her heart, but the silver stallion didn't shy or even look back over his shoulder.

Despite the nearby fire, Sam felt cold.

The Phantom should have bolted or even wheeled around to charge. She'd seen him do that to Jake under much less stressful conditions. But the stallion had given no sign of fear, rage, or even annoyance.

The ever-alert mustang only stared into the pasture and gave a long, melancholy neigh.

The second time Dr. Scott clapped his hands, Sam wasn't startled. She was heartsick.

She knew what the vet was doing. He was giving her horse a test, and the great gray stallion had failed.

"I don't think he can hear us," Dr. Scott said softly. "Sam, I'm afraid the explosion has made the Phantom deaf."

Chapter Eight ↜

𝒯he Phantom pawed rapidly, scoring the black ground with his mark.

He looked kingly and tough. Sam knew Dr. Scott had to be wrong.

But then the Phantom wheeled right. He gathered himself and burst into a trot, but he'd just begun his circle when he saw them. And shied. He hadn't heard them right behind him.

Sam noticed more than his surprise.

"His neck," Sam gasped.

The stallion hadn't escaped the fire without burns. A scorch on the right side of his neck had the crumpled and cratered surface of a toasted marshmallow.

"Oh, no," Dr. Scott snapped. "Why didn't I move in and sedate him when I had the chance? It's not going to be easy, now."

The stallion's startled stepping in place stopped as Dr. Scott bent to withdraw a hypodermic syringe from his bag. Maybe the vet suddenly looked like a four-legged predator, or maybe the Phantom was out of patience with humans. However he came to his decision, the stallion hopped over the burned section of fence and dashed after his herd, without a backward glance for Pirate.

The young horse shuddered a little. Even unconscious, could he know he'd been abandoned?

"I'm not going to make the same mistake with this one," Dr. Scott muttered.

As he set to work on Pirate, Sam looked after the Phantom.

Deaf, she thought. A shuddering sigh passed her lips. What happened to a deaf horse on the open range? She longed to ask Dr. Scott, but not now.

Dr. Scott's movements were brisk. Was he angry or just efficient as he jabbed the needle into the small bottle of liquid?

He finished filling the syringe, then strode to the trembling horse. The vet dropped to one knee beside Pirate.

"I'll have to catch him and examine him later," the young vet said. He was injecting medicine into Pirate, but Sam knew he was talking about the Phantom.

"The important thing now is for me to help this young one."

With gentle hands, Dr. Scott examined Pirate.

"Why is he unconscious?" Sam asked.

"Shock," Dr. Scott said. "I gave him a sedative. Not much, though. With this facial swelling from burns and smoke inhalation, I don't want to compromise his respiration any further."

Pirate's head looked disproportionately big, so Sam was relieved to hear the colt's face was swollen for the same reasons she was rubbing her eyes and sniffing through a nose that felt twice its normal size.

Dr. Scott's hand hovered above the light patch surrounding the colt's eye. It was red, instead of white. Was the skin beneath the white hair more delicate? The vet frowned with such intense concentration, Sam kept her question for later.

"I'm going to need a hand getting him into the horse ambulance," the vet said, then shook his head. "I hate to take him away from everything he knows. I'll put another horse with him at the clinic, but he won't like waking up without his band."

"Will he be all right?" Sam asked, finally.

The vet's lips pressed in a hard line. His eyes seemed to add up each detail of the colt's condition and calculate his chances.

"Do you know what 'guarded condition' means?" the vet asked.

She mulled the words over for a few seconds,

then guessed, "Like bad, but it could get worse?"

"Yeah." Dr. Scott sounded discouraged. "We need to get this hole in the fence closed up, too, or we could be dealing with more injuries."

Sam looked at Mrs. Allen's fence. It wouldn't stop the Phantom if he decided to run for home. And he *would* want out, as soon as he recovered. Wouldn't he?

"He could jump it," Sam said.

"Let's hope he doesn't want to," Dr. Scott said, packing up his bag.

Despair puffed up inside Sam's chest, making it hard for her to breathe. Smoke inhalation was nothing compared to this feeling. She'd never seen the silver stallion choose fences over freedom. It was unthinkable. Ace had, and after she'd foaled, so had Dark Sunshine—but not the Phantom.

Out in the pasture, he glimmered in the smoky gloom, bright as the sun that glowed through the haze overhead. She didn't like thinking how hard it would be to bring the stallion in for examination, but at least he was near enough that she could watch over him.

Dr. Scott looked down at Pirate and shook his head. Then he squinted toward the firefighters.

"Luke," Dr. Scott called. He shouted twice more before he got Jake's dad's attention. "We need a quick repair on this fence. I'm not set up to do it until I go back, and . . ."

Jake's dad gave an okay sign and right away, Jake and Bryan swarmed out of the truck.

"We gotcha handled," Bryan said as they hurried toward the ruined section of fence, then stretched yellow "fire scene" tape back and forth between the fence posts.

"They can walk right through this, I know." Bryan took out a pocket knife as he talked to the vet. "But I'll cut off some short pieces and tie 'em on here so they'll flutter in the wind and maybe spook 'em back."

"Good idea," Dr. Scott said. It was the first time Sam had seen him smile all day. "Nice workin' with folks who know stock," he added.

As Sam's eyes strayed over the blackened grass and weeds, she noticed something made of crumpled metal. It took her a few minutes to realize she was looking at one of the paint cans. How much of the damage was from the explosion and how much had it melted from the fire's heat?

Pirate had been right next to it. No wonder he lay so still.

And the Phantom . . .

"'Bout time you showed up." Dr. Scott's grumble broke Sam's trance. "I called you as soon as I heard. Now, I need some help loading this colt."

It was a pained intake of breath that made Sam look up. She knew it was her horse-loving step-mother before she saw Brynna's saddened face.

"Are we going to lose him?" Brynna asked, looking down at Pirate.

"Not if I've got your permission to treat him," the vet said. He raised one brow and Sam knew Pirate's care would be expensive.

Brynna didn't hesitate. Sam felt a flood of relief and love as Brynna said, "Do it."

Sam rushed to Brynna, who put an arm around her shoulders. They stood together as Bryan, Jake, and the BLM worker Sam thought of as Bale Tosser helped Dr. Scott maneuver Pirate into the trailer.

"Keep your eyes open for trouble," he instructed Sam, as he nodded toward the huge pasture. "I'll be back to check out the rest of them, as soon as I've got this guy stabilized."

As soon as the vet's tires crunched, moving away, Brynna enclosed Sam in a hug.

The creases in Brynna's khaki uniform were sharp and Sam could feel the edge of the official name tag pinned to her crisp shirt. Brynna's hair had been scraped back, then braided so the corners of her eyes showed its tightness, but there was nothing professional about Brynna's hug. It told Sam she was loved.

"I'm okay," Sam said, her voice muffled against Brynna's neck. "Nothing's wrong with *me*."

"I can see that now," Brynna managed, setting Sam back at arm's length. "But I've been on an emotional roller coaster for the last thirty minutes. First, the emergency radio only called out the volunteer fire department's brush truck." She nodded at the vehicle. "The fire sounded like a tiny flare-up, so, even when

Dr. Scott called BLM to let me know there could be wild horses involved, I wasn't worried. Neither was Wyatt, or he never would have stayed home. You know that."

If his new baby had been near a brush fire . . . Sam shook the jealous thought from her head. She was fourteen years old and in charge of an entire ranch. She should be able to handle an emergency like this.

And she had. It was a good thing Brynna couldn't read minds, because that resentful notion had been just plain stupid.

". . . closer I got, the worse it looked. Then, I passed Callie on the road—"

"Is she okay?" Sam interrupted.

"She looked fine to me," Brynna said. "Where was she headed with that trailer?"

"Our ranch," Sam said.

In her instant of hesitation, Brynna must have thought of Dad, then the money for extra hay, and finally, Western hospitality.

"Oh," Brynna said, shrugging. "All right."

Sam nodded. If Brynna was satisfied, was there really any reason to mention Imp and Angel? Sam decided there wasn't. She'd find out soon enough.

"Of course, I wondered why Callie was evacuating horses, but it wasn't until I got close enough to see flames . . ." Brynna bit her lip, then shook off the memory and smiled. "That was about the same time Sheriff Ballard closed the road."

"He closed the road?" Sam asked. She could imagine the mustached sheriff, arms crossed and boots set apart as he stood beside his black-and-white police car. "How did you get through?"

"I pestered and threatened him until he realized I'd start a riot if he didn't let me past."

"Not really," Sam said skeptically. How could one small woman start a riot?

"No, not really, but there were lots of good Samaritans lined up with trailers, willing to rescue the sanctuary horses, who didn't like being kept out."

"Like who?" Sam asked.

Brynna rattled off a list of local ranchers, including Jed Kenworthy, Jen's dad, who had once scoffed at Mrs. Allen's sanctuary. He couldn't believe she'd waste money on such "good for nothin'" animals, but out here, neighborliness came first.

"By the time I reminded Heck Ballard I was a peace officer, too," Brynna said, "he was ready to just wave me on through."

Brynna let out a sigh. When she drew a breath to replace it, she coughed. Suddenly Sam remembered the baby. She'd been careful of each mouthful Dark Sunshine had eaten while she was in foal. She should be just as protective of Brynna, even if the whole situation made her uneasy.

"Should you be here?" Sam asked. When Brynna looked hurt, she asked, "Breathing the smoke and everything? You know?"

Once Brynna understood, her expression softened. "Thanks, honey, but I think I'll be okay. Besides, it's my job to look after the horses. Did you say we have an entire band out there? Were any others hurt?"

"The Phantom," Sam said.

Brynna's mouth opened in horror. She looked around, searching for something she dreaded seeing.

"He's in there, with the rest of his herd," Sam rushed on. If she stopped to take in Brynna's sympathy, she'd start crying. And she wasn't about to do that. "He's burned and Dr. Scott thinks he might be deaf from the explosion—"

"Explosion? Was it the propane tank? Something left over from mining? My gosh, the house—"

Sam interrupted her. "It was from the paint cans I left out near the fence."

Guilt avalanched down on Sam. She hadn't had time to feel it, until now.

Sure, Mrs. Allen had talked her into leaving them there, but Mrs. Allen hadn't been here this morning when lightning had struck.

If I'd only thought, Sam realized, *I could have prevented Pirate's injury and the Phantom's.*

"That's an unlucky coincidence," Brynna said sternly, as if she could keep Sam from feeling guilty. "But that's all. And almost certainly it will be temporary."

Temporary? Sam felt as if Brynna had boosted her into the sky.

"Are you sure? How do you know?" Sam wanted to believe it, but what if Brynna was wrong?

"Because it was a minor explosion. That doesn't mean you won't have some waiting to do."

"I can wait," Sam said, and already she imagined herself, back propped against the pasture fence, reading while the Phantom stood nearby.

Then Brynna interrupted her daydream. "Do you think I should evacuate them all to Willow Springs?" Brynna asked.

Sam caught her breath. As always, Brynna trusted her instincts about horses, but this time the burden was heavier than usual.

The mustangs would be safer at Willow Springs, but once there, it would be simple to vaccinate and freeze-brand the horses, then put them up for adoption. And she wanted them to stay free.

She tried to focus on Brynna's question, though, instead of letting her feelings run away with her.

"I don't think we'll need to evacuate," she said, sensibly. "If the fire doesn't turn back this way, they're okay here. I have to stay and watch Mrs. Allen's place, anyhow, so I'll keep watch. Besides, Callie will be back."

At the mention of Callie, Brynna's mouth tightened in a straight line. She gave her head a small disapproving shake.

"What?" Sam asked. She knew Brynna had

approved Callie's adoption of Queen. And she'd thought it was okay for the two of them to take care of Mrs. Allen's ranch. So what was she frowning about?

"Nothing." Brynna said. "Or if—" She shook her head again. "It can wait. Right now I'll go talk with Luke and the chief from Darton and see if they can predict what this fire will do next."

Brynna took a small leather-bound notebook from her pocket.

"If all their graze was burned off," she said, eyes doing a quick assessment of the terrain, "I'd board them here and arrange to pay Trudy for their food, but I don't think it will be necessary. It looks like there's still plenty to eat.

"Besides, if we keep them off their territory for too long—well, you know how wild horses can be. That black horse you call Moon will be back, or another stallion just like him, and the Phantom will have a fight on his hands. Hooves, I mean," Brynna amended, smiling as she closed her notebook.

Brynna was trying to joke about it, but could the Phantom battle another stallion in silence? Every snort and neigh was a clue to his opponent's weakness. If he couldn't hear them, he'd be handicapped.

Sam swallowed hard and looked into her stepmother's eyes.

"Ask me," Brynna said.

Even though she'd just brushed aside the other

question, Sam knew Brynna could tell this one was serious. Brynna would answer, if Sam could get up the guts to ask.

Sam wet her lips, drew in a breath, then let it out. "What if his deafness is permanent? Would you release his herd without him?"

Chapter Nine ❧

ℬrynna's eyes widened, but then she looked away, staring out into the pasture. There wasn't a horse in sight.

"Since he's an adult horse and knows what to watch for on the range, I'm sure he'd survive," Brynna said slowly, "but I'd need to do some research."

"Do you think he'd still be a leader?" Sam knew it wasn't a fair question, but Brynna was a biologist. She'd explain the truth, no matter how ugly.

"It's unlikely," Brynna said. "Horses interpret what's around them with sight, smell, and sound. He'd be missing a full third of what he needs to know about his world."

Sam thought of her own world. If it were divided

into three parts, there'd be her family, horses, and her friends. Which third could she do without?

She couldn't choose. And the Phantom hadn't been allowed to choose.

"Herd stallions are always on guard," Brynna added. "Without his full alarm system, his herd wouldn't be as safe."

"But mustangs don't talk that much," Sam protested.

"You mean neighs and whinnies," Brynna said.

"Yeah, they move their heads and tails and ears and eyes, right? The Phantom would still have all that."

"He would," Brynna said. "But I think you may be getting all worked up about something that won't even be an issue this time tomorrow.

"As long as I'm out here," Brynna continued, "I want to check the herd and see if we've got any other injuries, or any strays. After I talk with the fire chiefs, I'll come right back and we'll saddle up."

It would have been fun, riding out to check on the Phantom's herd as they mingled with Mrs. Allen's mustangs, but Sam couldn't be excited. She was too afraid she'd find the Phantom in misery.

"You're looking pretty flushed," Brynna said, touching Sam's cheek with the back of her hand. "Why don't you go inside and cool off while I do business. I'll meet you at the house as soon as I'm finished."

An oasis couldn't have felt more welcome than the

garden path up to Mrs. Allen's front door. Inside, Sam understood why Mrs. Allen always kept the drapes drawn. It was as good as air-conditioning, even though she didn't like the darkness.

Alone in Mrs. Allen's house, Sam wasn't sure what to do. It was awful quiet without the patter of the little dog feet.

Sam looked at the kitchen clock. It was only 3:30. Had it been just this morning that she and Callie arrived? And just three hours ago that they'd been making a lunch to take to the tree house? If it had been a school day, she'd just be getting home and putting on clothes in which she could do chores, then ride.

She glanced around the house for chores. Mrs. Allen had left her house tidier than usual. Sam imagined her filling the hours until she could drive to the airport by scrubbing the kitchen sink and counters, vacuuming, dusting, and arranging her bills into neat stacks. Even the dogs' dishes were shiny and arranged on a scrubbed plastic mat.

If Imp and Angel had been sniffing around her ankles, she'd feel less like an intruder, Sam thought.

Had Mrs. Allen called? She didn't have an answering machine, so there was no way to tell. Maybe she'd called Gram with news she didn't want to share with kids.

Her grandson's legs wouldn't move. What was his name? The least she could do was remember. Sam concentrated. Was it Josh? No . . . Gideon? Wait,

Gabriel, that was it! She'd bet his friends called him Gabe.

Poor Gabriel, who had just gotten his driver's license, could be paralyzed.

Sam shuddered. He was only two years older than she was. Younger than Jake. What would it be like to never mount a horse, or run after a friend or stand on a chair to reach a high shelf again? But maybe the condition was temporary, like the Phantom's.

One thing was sure: Gabriel's accident had reduced the importance of her jealousy over Dad and Brynna's baby to a speck of dust.

To be fair, it wasn't Brynna she was mad at. If she was mad at anyone, it was Dad. She couldn't blame Brynna for wanting a child of her own, but Dad already had one.

She was his child. They'd been family for thirteen years before he fell in love with Brynna. And hadn't she been pretty tolerant of his new wife? Sam asked herself. Not perfect, maybe, but better than a lot of kids.

Why hadn't he taken her aside and talked with her about this? Why hadn't he let her get mad at him instead of spilling this big news, then sending her away? Of course he hadn't planned this, but . . .

But he *hadn't*.

And he probably had a perfectly good reason for not showing up to check on her, while she was surrounded by the towering flames of a wildfire.

"Act your age," Sam mumbled.

She'd started worrying over Gabriel, and ended up feeling sorry for herself. If that wasn't immature, what was?

Gram always said the quickest way to stop feeling sad was to quit thinking about how tough you had it, and do something nice for someone else.

And that someone had to be Brynna.

Even though she hadn't said anything mean to her stepmother, Sam wanted to make up for her jealousy.

Picking one of Mrs. Allen's flowers for her stepmother was lame.

Coffee, Sam thought. Brynna loved good coffee, and Sam was standing right in the middle of Mrs. Allen's kitchen, so she'd make her a cup. Even though it was hot outside, it was cool enough inside that she'd appreciate it.

As she ran water into the kettle, Sam noticed her hands were black with grime from the fire. She finished setting up the drip coffeepot, then ducked into the downstairs bathroom to wash up.

Mirrored over the bathroom sink, she looked ready for Halloween. It was bad enough that soot and smoke smeared her face, but tears had channeled through the gray grunge. Her hair added to the look by sticking up in random clumps in a way Jake had once said made her look like a chrysanthemum.

Sam stuck out her tongue at her reflection, then

set to work until the tea kettle whistled for attention.

Gently she poured the hot water over the ground coffee. She let it drip while she looked for some kind of snack. She was sure Mrs. Allen wouldn't mind.

In one kitchen drawer, she found an opened package of chocolate sandwich cookies. Six were left, so she arranged them on a plate she found in a cupboard, next to a blue pottery mug with black speckles. She'd just poured coffee into the mug when Brynna came inside with the scent of smoke clinging to her clothes.

"I made you some coffee," Sam said, extending the mug.

"I can't drink it," Brynna said. She took a long step back as if Sam had offered her poison. "It smells wonderful and I wish I could, but it's bad for the baby."

"Oh," Sam said, looking into the dark-brown liquid.

"But I would love some ice water, and I'll make some, right after I fix this up for you." Brynna took the cup back to the kitchen counter. She opened Mrs. Allen's refrigerator, surveyed the contents for a minute, then removed a short carton. "Real cream," she said, then glanced at the date on its side, before pouring a silken stream into the cup. She added two heaping spoons of sugar, then handed Sam the cup. "See what you think."

It was amazingly good.

"Wow," Sam told Brynna. "You're going to have

to start making this for me every morning."

"Dream on," Brynna joked, but Sam could tell her stepmother was pleased.

From outside, there was a beeping sound, the kind of beep that says a truck is backing up and you'd better watch out or get run over. The fire trucks must be leaving the ranch.

"What did Luke say?" Sam asked.

"Luke told me the fire is 'knocked down' on this side of the river, so the horses can stay here," Brynna said, once she held her glass of ice water.

"Good," Sam said with a sigh.

"But the fire jumped the La Charla—"

It was a long, winding river, but one thought flashed through Sam's mind.

"River Bend—!"

"—is okay as far as I know," Brynna said. "I couldn't get an answer on my cell phone," Brynna said, "but that's no big surprise."

Sam nodded. Not only were Gram and Dad out of the house as often as they were in, but telephone reception was unpredictable. It rarely mattered, but it could be maddening in an emergency.

"Should you leave? I can check the horses myself," Sam offered.

"There's no point in it," Brynna said. "Luke says Heck Ballard's moved his road block and he's only allowing emergency vehicles through." Brynna shrugged as if it didn't matter, but Sam saw her concern. "Luke called it a crown fire. I guess sparks blew as far as Aspen Creek and burned from treetop to treetop. He says it's an unpredictable kind of fire, but not nearly as serious here as it would be lots of places."

"'Cause we don't have that many trees," Sam agreed, but she thought of the cottonwoods' shade along the river, and the few in their ranch yard. "I guess it's a good thing Dad stayed home."

And it explained why Dad still hadn't shown up.

Brynna cleared her throat and gave a decisive nod, almost as if she didn't want to talk. Was she afraid her voice would come out sounding shaky and worried?

Twenty minutes later, Ace and Judge were saddled. Sam and Brynna were ready to ride out and see if any of the mustangs needed treatment.

"This'll be fun," Brynna said with a hint of sarcasm, as she swung aboard Judge. Mrs. Allen's elderly bay had fought each step of being saddled. Now he stood with nostrils distended, sucking in smoky air. After each breath he gave a high-pitched whinny.

"Want me to ride him?" Sam asked, though she was already mounted on Ace.

"Of course not," Brynna said. She leaned forward to give the old gelding's neck a pat. "We'll do fine. Won't we, Judge?"

Brynna reined the bay away from Ace, and jogged toward the big open pasture. As Sam followed, she found herself worrying about the baby again.

Brynna was an excellent rider and she knew the nature of horses, but accidents could happen. If Judge surprised her, and she fell, would she hurt the baby?

Sam blew her cheeks full of air, impatient with herself. If she kept up this paranoia, she'd be a basket case by January.

"Efficient guys," Brynna said, nodding toward the sound of pounding hammers.

The truck she'd heard leaving must have been the one from Darton, because the volunteer fire truck, and firefighters, were still there.

Dressed in fireman's yellow, Jake and Quinn nailed up boards to replace the fire scene tape they'd wound around the fence posts. Sam wondered, just for a minute, where they'd found the scrap lumber to do the job.

When she remembered the woodpile behind the barn, Sam thought of the snakes they'd had in their woodpile at River Bend. What if snakes fleeing the fire had taken refuge in Mrs. Allen's woodpile?

Sam shuddered and vowed to keep her eyes open. She liked snakes fine, if they stayed far away from her.

Just now, though, she had other things to worry over.

Sam sucked her stomach in so hard it ached as they passed through the pasture gate. There must be fear in this smoke, she thought, because it had been months since she'd remembered her accident as she rode through a gate.

Now she imagined falling, impact against her skull, and the sound of fading hoofbeats.

"Quit dawdling, Ace." She scolded the bay gelding, and tightened her legs so he moved to catch up with Judge.

"Look who's coming to see us," Brynna said.

Sleek and swift as a Thoroughbred, the cocoa-brown horse was easy to recognize.

Apache Hotspot, Linc Slocum's blue-blooded Appaloosa mare, had been stolen by the Phantom just a few weeks ago. Now she loped toward them, as if she'd had enough of freedom.

Ace's head flew up and Sam felt exhilaration course through the gelding. If she didn't keep Ace reined in, he'd bolt to greet Hotspot. A glance told Sam that Brynna was gathering Judge's reins tighter as well.

Just yards away, Hotspot swerved away, but she looked over her shoulder, past her milky body and white tail, watching the riders come closer.

"She's still wearing her halter," Sam noticed.

"Yes, I think she's all dressed up to go home," Brynna said.

Brynna was joking, but Hotspot's solitary greeting gave Sam a bad feeling.

The Appaloosa mare had been running with the Phantom's herd. Even though she was stable bred, shouldn't she want to stick with the band now, when she'd just been through a frightening experience?

"Those blood bays are from his herd, too," Brynna said as two grazing mustangs noticed the riders and galloped away.

Was the Phantom's herd falling apart?

Sam gritted her teeth. Ace's gait turned from a fluid jog to a jolting, uncomfortable trot, as if despair had telegraphed down the reins.

Sam tried not to lose hope, but she was afraid. These scattered horses might be telling her the Phantom's power was gone.

Chapter Ten ❧

*I*t was a long time until they saw another horse.

Sam's legs felt raw inside her jeans. It must've been droplets from the fire hoses that had made the old, soft denim chafe.

Her nose was stuffy and her sinuses, just above her eyebrows, hurt. She thought of Pirate's swollen face. Breathing smoke was just plain bad for everyone and she didn't know how firefighters lived with it.

As they splashed through puddles, Sam realized that the storm that Blaze's howls and the spinning spider had predicted had just been a cloudburst, but it had changed everything.

They rode up a sagebrush slope, and Hotspot tagged along, refusing to be left behind.

"Do you suppose I should call Mrs. Allen and tell her everything's all right?" Sam asked Brynna. "If she saw a report on television, she might worry."

"I doubt it was big enough to be covered in Denver," Brynna said. "It seems huge to us because it's our home, but other people assume there's nothing out here," Brynna shrugged. "Trudy will be calling you soon, anyway."

"She will?" Sam asked. She knew Mrs. Allen would ask about Imp and Angel, and Sam hoped they'd be back by then.

"Your gram talked with her early this morning. Nothing has changed with her grandson so far. They're worried and waiting."

Sam swallowed hard and looked at the range ahead. Dusk was coming. It was hard to tell through the lingering smoke.

"Let's check the drop-off," Brynna said.

Sam shivered at the reminder of the night they'd searched for Faith. Mrs. Allen had sent the adults looking in this direction, because of the dangerous terrain. During some ancient flood, the river had carved off a piece of land and left a steep drop-off down to the riverbank.

"That's not so bad," Sam said once they drew rein at the edge. A narrow path, wide enough for a single horse, led down the La Charla River. "Although, in a snowstorm—"

"You could blunder right off the edge," Brynna

finished. "Good thing she's got a fence on the other side."

Sam agreed. Now, the La Charla was running fairly high, but by late summer it would be no barrier to the horses.

"Looks like they've been here," Brynna added, and Sam saw the fresh imprints of many hooves in the damp sandy soil around the base of a string of willow trees.

They rode on.

Ace shied when Brynna raised the left hand that had rested on her thigh as they rode. Judge shambled to a stop and Sam looked ahead.

Both mustang herds were in disarray.

Belle grazed alongside the mare Fourteen and her colt Windfall, but Faith had ventured away to extend her sniffing nose toward Sugar, the Phantom's roan filly and a wild yellow dun. When the wild mustangs ignored her, Faith twitched her dark-gold ears toward a movement acres away.

The sightless filly had sensed the Phantom. He glowed moon silver, far to the left of most of the scattered horses. Flanked by Queen and his honey-brown lead mare, Sam wondered why he still looked so alone.

The stallion circled in a small area no bigger than a basketball court. His head swung from side to side, but he was on level ground. He couldn't be on guard. In fact, he didn't look at anything for more than a second.

"He couldn't have gone blind, too. Could he?" Sam asked, horrified by the stallion's vague, out-of-touch manner.

"He's in shock," Brynna whispered.

An ache spread from Sam's breastbone. It wrapped around her chest to her spine, like a thick iron band.

Poor sweet Blackie, Sam thought. As a foal, he'd looked this lost on the day he'd been weaned. Something had been taken from him, and he couldn't understand why.

All at once, he broke into a determined trot, crossing to greet one of Mrs. Allen's horses, a sorrel filly with the twisted legs. She froze to attention, eyes wide, nostrils flared. The Phantom snorted his breath into her nostrils, and moved on to Licorice. The black mare trembled, but she stood still for the Phantom's inspection, letting him sniff along her back before he moved on to Belle.

Clearly uneasy, the paint mare swung her haunches to bump a curious foal away. Still, Belle recognized the Phantom as a superior, and she accepted his greeting and returned it with a snort of her own.

"That's what would happen in the wild," Brynna said softly, "if he came across mares without a herd stallion. Look at Roman. He can't decide if he should challenge."

The liver-chestnut gelding stood under a tall cottonwood tree, watching. From the first day the adopted mustangs had been herded from Willow Springs Wild Horse Center to Deerpath Ranch, he had been the boss.

With his long mane and untrimmed hair under his cheeks and chin, Roman looked primitive and fierce, but the Phantom was a tested range stallion and Roman seemed to know it.

Motionless, Roman watched the stallion examine each captive mustang. When a branch above him creaked in the hot wind, Roman shied. He'd been that intent.

Tension in the captive herd made the horses near the Phantom start to quarrel. Ears flattened. Teeth flashed. They were ready for this scrutiny to end.

Finally, Roman neighed a protest at the Phantom's intrusion. The silver stallion didn't notice. He continued sniffing Windfall's ears.

"Oh no. He didn't hear that," Sam said, worried.

Brynna nodded, and her reddish eyebrows lowered in a frown.

The lack of a response made Roman brave. A forefoot struck out. His neck arched and he pranced toward the Phantom.

Though he hadn't heard, the Phantom saw the movement. He shook his heavy mane, turned his tail to Roman, and moved away, slow as a sleepwalker.

"He's not giving up," Sam said.

"No, but Roman doesn't—"

Before Brynna could finish, Roman charged toward the Phantom, stopping short in a half rear which raised his head above the stallion's in a move to show his dominance.

The Phantom must have felt the earth shake from the gelding's charge, because he swung around in time to see Roman's rear.

At a weary trot, the Phantom returned to face the liver chestnut. Ears tilted forward, the silver stallion signaled he'd meant no harm. When Roman kept his ears pinned and rose in a second rear, the Phantom rumbled a low neigh, reared even higher, and came down hard on the gelding's back.

Though Roman had fallen to his knees, the Phantom didn't continue the attack.

"He's not even trying," Sam said.

"I know," Brynna answered.

They'd seen the Phantom battle other stallions before. This action was only a warning.

He had no interest in claiming Roman's herd. The silver stallion proved it by wheeling and loping away, to stand alone with his head lowered.

"He might do all right on the range, even if he couldn't hear," Sam said, but she didn't even convince herself.

The Phantom might rule inside pasture fences.

Free, he wouldn't face uncertain geldings like Roman. Last spring he'd beaten young stallions like New Moon and Yellow Tail, but as each day of summer passed, they grew stronger and smarter.

"That horse couldn't have a better friend than you," Brynna said suddenly.

"I don't know," Sam said. "I was just about to take back what I said. I'm not sure he would survive on the range."

"That's why I think you're his best friend. Most of the time, people see something wild and beautiful and their impulse is to tame it. It never occurs to them that they're taking away what makes it beautiful. But you don't feel like that, do you?"

"No," Sam said. "There's like this magic connection between us—"

"Okay, stop right there," Brynna said. "That's what I wanted to talk with you about earlier. You and the Phantom do have a special relationship, but it's a bond based on good horse handling, not magic."

"I didn't exactly mean—"

"Wyatt told me you slept in his stall on the night he was born. Today they'd call that imprinting. And you gentled him, rather than breaking him."

"Jake had a lot to do with the way I trained him," Sam said.

"Right, and I've read the literature, Sam. There's nothing mystical about Native American horse training. It considers horses' minds, the fact that they're prey animals, herd animals . . ." Brynna paused to draw a breath, and she must have seen Sam's surprise at her tirade.

"I'm sorry for going off like that, but I don't want you to be taken in with Callie's mystical nonsense."

Sam thought of Callie loading two horses and two dogs in ten minutes. She thought of the way she'd backed the unfamiliar trailer and left the ranch, without panicking the animals. She pictured Queen, a wild lead mare, treating Callie as a friend.

If Callie had used mystical nonsense on those animals, it had worked.

"How can you say that?" Sam asked. "She's doing great with Queen."

"She may be," Brynna said, "but she believes in magic crystals and that sort of hocus-pocus." Brynna turned Judge back toward the ranch house before she added, "And she's a vegetarian."

Sam slapped her brow, then realized how lucky she was that Ace hadn't shied in protest. Maybe he was following the conversation, too.

"Brynna! You're the one who suggested Callie help me over here!"

Sam couldn't believe the way Brynna was talking. Her stepmother was smarter than this.

"I know, but I ran into Jed Kenworthy at Clara's this morning before work—"

"Oh, good," Sam said, and if she rolled her eyes in frustration, she didn't care.

Sam liked her best friend's father. He knew more about horses than she ever would, but he could be intolerant and closed-minded. She'd once overheard him talking to Dad, saying he didn't know what Luke Ely was thinking, letting his boys wear their hair every which way, one like a hippie—that would be Jake, Sam knew—and one like a punk.

Brynna looked a little sheepish.

"I know being a vegetarian doesn't guarantee you're weird—"

"Except in Nevada," Sam grumbled. She loved this open-range state, but she wasn't proud of some of its quirks. "But I'll tell you my darkest secret." Sam lowered her voice as if she were confiding a crime. "I've eaten tofu. And bean sprouts."

Brynna laughed then, and Sam could tell she was mostly laughing at herself.

"Okay, you're right, I'm a little judgmental when it comes to people's relationships with animals. I want them treated with respect for themselves—not like they're furry people."

Sam laughed, too, but insisted, "Callie respects Queen, and even though she talks about their mystical bond, Callie mostly just pays really close attention to Queen's reactions."

"The same way you do with horses," Brynna said.

"Yep," Sam said, and then crossed her fingers that this conversation was over.

❄ ❄ ❄

It was almost dark when they reached the house. Sam saw that Callie's Jeep and the trailer were back. When she and Brynna had cooled down the horses and stripped them of tack, Brynna tried to call Dad on her cell phone.

Apparently, it didn't work.

"Stupid thing," Brynna said. She stared at the phone as if she could jump-start it with brain waves. When it didn't respond, she decided to use Mrs. Allen's phone.

Light streamed from the open door down the garden path. Callie stood in the doorway with crossed arms. In the dim light, her hair looked dusty pink instead of magenta.

"I was just about to come get you," Callie said. "Your . . ." Callie hesitated, looking from Sam to Brynna. "Wyatt called."

It was Brynna who hustled into Mrs. Allen's kitchen first.

"It *is* sort of late," she muttered.

Smiling, Callie looked after Brynna. She didn't seem offended that Brynna hadn't at least said, *Hi Callie, haven't seen you for a long time,* or something like that.

As the older girl turned, Sam noticed Callie's hair was shaved up her neck, leaving just the sides long, and for some reason her nape looked vulnerable.

"Are you okay?" Callie asked. A bracelet hung

with tiny brass bells tinkled on her wrist as she touched Sam's shoulder. "And Queen?"

Callie's voice quavered, and Sam could see how worried she was.

"She's fine, and she's keeping the Phantom company. He really needs her right now."

"The Phantom? She's with him?" Callie's gray eyes rounded behind her glasses and Sam knew she must be imagining her mare's return to the range.

"They're in the pasture," Sam said.

Even though the words threatened to drain off the last of her energy, Sam found herself telling Callie about the burned fence, Pirate, the Phantom, and everything else, until Brynna's voice sharpened, drawing their attention.

"What little dogs?" Brynna said into the telephone receiver, but her eyebrows arched as she looked at Callie and Sam. "Oh, really? I just bet." Brynna winced. "Well, those living room drapes were due to be replaced anyway."

"Uh-oh," Sam said. Brynna told Dad she'd be home soon, then hung up.

"Cougar isn't enjoying his new roommates," Brynna said. "Apparently he ran up the drapes and won't come down. Wyatt says the way Cougar's lashing his tail and yowling, there's no way he's going to reach up there for him."

"I can go right back over," Callie began, looking contrite.

"Don't think of it," Brynna said, waving away the suggestion. "It was the right thing to do, taking the dogs over there. Firefighters are injured all the time going after pets.

"Besides, with Sam over here, we'll probably get bored and need a little excitement," Brynna joked. "I'll bring them home tomorrow.

"There was something else I was supposed to tell you," Brynna said, fanning herself with her hand. "What was it . . . Oh, Callie."

Callie's face lit with a mild smile.

That's the difference between us, Sam thought. If Brynna said, "Oh, Sam," she'd assume she'd done something wrong.

"Yes?"

"It seems you talked with Sheriff Ballard?"

Callie shrugged. "I just thanked him for getting out here so quickly, and helping to get the fire trucks through."

"Well, whatever you told him, helped, because he talked with Clara at the coffee shop and she sent out free food for the firefighters."

"Great," Callie said.

"Not only that, Clara mentioned the wild horses to Phil at Phil's Fill-Up and Feed, and he's sending out some free hay to supplement Trudy's grass."

"Wow!" Sam said.

"And Phil told his daughter about the graze being burned off and I guess her scout leader is talking about organizing some kind of reseeding project."

"All that from telling Sheriff Ballard 'thank you'?" Sam asked, and when she took in Brynna's and Callie's expressions, she saw that one wore a warning and the other a grin.

"Call it karma, the Golden Rule, whatever," Callie said, "but it means the same thing in any society— what goes around, comes around."

As Callie gave a satisfied nod and moved toward the kitchen, Brynna pulled Sam along with her to the door.

"Quit looking so smug," Brynna whispered, with a glance back at Callie. "This is something serious."

"Okay."

"I think your horse could be dangerous tonight. By tomorrow he could be hearing—"

"And gone," Sam said, crossing her fingers.

"That, or he might have settled down. But it's better to be safe than sorry. Give him some space. You saw how he told Roman to back off," Brynna said. "You don't want him to do the same to you."

He wouldn't, Sam thought, but she said, "Okay, but I'll be out there as soon as I wake up."

"I figured you would be," Brynna said, but then Callie's voice floated to them from inside.

"Sam, did the Phantom like carrots when he was a colt? I brought the ingredients to make carrot crispies and they just might cheer him up."

"Don't forget what I told you," Brynna said,

rolling her eyes meaningfully toward the kitchen.

"I won't," Sam said. "No mystical nonsense."

Just the same, Sam was remembering two things Brynna had said, too.

She wouldn't treat the Phantom like a furry person, but she would be his very best friend.

Chapter Eleven ❧

Sam came back inside the house to see that Callie had grated a mound of carrots and apples. A bottle of dark-brown molasses and a bag of bran sat beside a box of crackers. With crossed arms, Callie considered the ingredients.

"Carrot crispies are horse cookies I make for Queen," Callie said, "and I know Ace will like them, but we might want to check with Dr. Scott about the Phantom."

"He might not be used to any of that stuff, but I'm sure he could eat it," Sam said.

"Maybe, but the Phantom's probably still in shock," Callie said, shaking her head. "When people are afraid, chemicals jolt through them so they can turn superalert, or escape. Their pulses and breathing speed up, and I think their blood sugar goes up. Some of that's got to be true for horses, too, and I'm looking at all the sugar in this—"

"I don't see any sugar," Sam said.

"The molasses, the carrots, and the apple have sugar in them," Callie pointed out.

"Oh, yeah. Just because it's not sitting there in a bag labeled 'sugar,' I forgot," Sam said. She felt her cheeks heat with a blush.

"Don't feel dumb," Callie said as she mixed the ingredients together. "I'm a vegetarian and I live alone. If I don't watch out for my nutrition, no one else will."

Sam was admiring Callie all over again when the phone rang.

They both stared at it, abruptly aware they were visitors here. This was Mrs. Allen's house, so the call was probably for her.

"We *are* the house sitters," Callie said, "so we'd better answer."

Sam did. "Hello?"

"Sam, it's Trudy."

For a second, Sam didn't believe it.

Mrs. Allen's voice was usually strident and bossy, but the person on the other end of the line sounded fragile. Her voice was faint as a dry leaf's flutter.

"Hi, Mrs. Allen," Sam said.

"Everything's all right there at home, I hope."

Mrs. Allen sounded as if the quiet peace of Deerpath Ranch was a comfort.

"Things are pretty much okay," Sam said. She made a helpless face at Callie, who held her hands apart in amazement.

Yeah, right, except a fire burned a few dozen acres of your ranch, injured some horses and, oh yeah, you don't mind if another herd of wild mustangs moves in, do you?

But Mrs. Allen had more important things to worry over, so Sam kept those details for later. She waited, listening to the long distance sounds humming over the line.

"I know you're afraid to ask, so I'll tell you," Mrs. Allen said, and though she only paused an instant and Sam didn't know Gabriel, her hand tightened on the phone in dread.

As she waited, Sam met Callie's eyes. She stood with all her fingers crossed.

"Gabe is awake and very unhappy."

Sam gave an okay sign, then waggled her hand back and forth. Callie seemed to understand that Gabriel was alive, but not yet out of danger.

"He shifts between being angry, then so sad it breaks your heart. The doctors are giving us lectures, talking about stages of *grief* as if he'd died or lost the use of his legs forever, when they know . . ." Mrs. Allen's voice wavered. "They know very well, the paralysis could be temporary."

Temporary. Just like, maybe, the Phantom's deafness.

"I really hope it is, Mrs. Allen," Sam said.

"He realizes he never appreciated his legs." Mrs. Allen gave a sad chuckle. "But who does? He talks about skateboarding, kicking a soccer ball, even how fast he'd run to class after the bell had rung. I told him he'll do all those things again, but he ignored me." Mrs. Allen sounded amazed. "Then, he told me he wished, if it had to happen, that the accident had happened after he'd been out to visit me and learned to ride a horse."

"I'm so sorry," Sam said.

"I assured him there's plenty of time." Mrs. Allen's tone hardened. "If not this summer, then next, he'll learn to ride. And I have said a thousand prayers that it's the truth."

Sam fumbled for something to say. "But you're right there with him, and he can tell you love him," Sam tried.

Mrs. Allen's heavy sigh came to Sam before the old woman said, "Love isn't magic, dear. If only it were."

If only, Sam thought.

Mrs. Allen cleared her throat. "Well, you hug those old horses and dogs for me, you hear, Samantha? My daughter's sleeping in a chair in Gabe's hospital room, but I need to put my old bones to bed or I won't be a bit of use to anyone tomorrow."

"Good night, Mrs. Allen. I'll think good thoughts."

Though it sounded lame to her, it was the only thing Sam could think to say.

"Thank you, dear," Mrs. Allen said wearily. "And you have pleasant dreams. Tell Callie and your family thank you all over again for me."

Sam hung up.

"You didn't tell her about the fire," Callie said.

"I know," Sam said, as if even she couldn't believe it herself. "But she was so sad already. Do you think that was wrong of me? Am I in trouble?"

"I don't know," Callie said. "I guess it doesn't change anything."

Sam recounted everything Mrs. Allen had said as she picked at the salad Callie had made, somehow, without her noticing.

"One thing she said that got to me was, 'Love isn't magic.'" Sam stopped and shook her head. "It makes me think how much I really, really want to help the Phantom, but I might not be able to do it."

"Isn't it kind of soon to give up?" Callie said.

"I'm not giving up," Sam insisted. "But I've read that lots of wild animals die when they get vet care, because contact with people traumatizes them as much as their injuries."

"That doesn't apply, here, for lots of reasons," Callie said. "Well, at least three." With both elbows on the kitchen table, Sam set her chin in her palms and waited for Callie to go on.

"First, the Phantom used to be domesticated, so he knows what this whole fences-and-hay thing is about," Callie said, holding up one finger. "Next, you know what he likes, so you can use your head to comfort him." Callie held up a third finger. "Most important, you have a special bond with him. Probably no one else in the world has that kind of connection with a wild horse!"

For a few seconds, Sam buried her face in her hands.

When she looked up, she gave a humorless laugh. "Do you know how sad that is? Our bond is a word. I gave him a secret name when he was my horse."

"That's not sad," Callie responded.

"It's really sad," Sam said, correcting her, "because he can't hear it anymore."

Callie sat back, spine pressed against her chair. "That's a good point, but your link with him is more than that," Callie said. "And if you're really going to be out in that pasture first thing tomorrow morning, like you told Brynna, we'd better get started making a plan."

Fire raged through Sam's dreams. Burning grass crackled and flared orange. Then, in the mysterious way of nightmares, the grass lengthened into stems, then monstrous flowers. Venus flytraps—brass yellow, red, and scarlet-gold—held their spiked lips closed, locking living things inside. She couldn't see what they were, but the things battered against the flowers' green-freckled throats, trying to escape, until the flowers blackened, curled, and sank into glowing embers.

Sam had never been so glad to wake up.

It was still so dark, she couldn't see the hand she held in front of her face, but that was okay. Heart pounding, mouth dry, Sam sat up, held the covers tight around herself, and stared into the shadows of Mrs. Allen's guest room.

Sam wished Imp and Angel were here, even though Callie breathed softly from the other twin bed.

Helplessness. That was a great thing to dream of before the sun rose on the most important day in her life with the Phantom.

Gradually, Sam made out the square box of the television and the wall-sized bookcase ridged with clothbound spines. She wished the walls boasted one of Mrs. Allen's early paintings of abstract wild horses, but she was thankful there were no portraits of carnivorous plants. They might sell like crazy in New York City, and Mrs. Allen might deserve the money she got from spending hours alone, painting in her studio, but those creepy creations made Sam nervous.

She ordered her brain to evict them from future dreams, and turned to her plan for today.

Since the stallion's hearing would have to heal itself, she and Callie had decided they could only reduce his fear. Today, they'd try to soothe him with food, music, and massage.

Hocus-pocus, Brynna might say, but once the stallion had stood in the La Charla River, listening to her sing Christmas carols, and Callie said she'd seen a television documentary about deaf children dancing to the vibrations they felt from music.

Massage made even more sense. The Phantom had allowed her to stroke her fingers through his mane until she had enough silver strands to weave a bracelet. He seemed to love her touch. But before she could touch him, she had to find him.

Sam inched her legs out from under the covers, trying not to disturb Callie.

Once she was on her feet, Sam lifted her duffel bag from the floor and tiptoed out, closing the bedroom door behind her.

Instead of coffee and roses, the living room held the smell of brush fire. Sam's throat ached from breathing it.

Putting her duffel bag on a chair, Sam edged the zipper down, tooth by tooth, and looked for her warm clothes. She knew she'd packed some. Even at the end of July, there were no guarantees in the high desert of northern Nevada. It could be a hundred degrees or twenty-five.

Sam pulled on socks, jeans, a short-sleeved T-shirt, and a long-sleeved flannel shirt. The flannel would be tied around her waist by breakfast time, but now she was chilly.

She tried to read the kitchen clock without flipping the light switch.

Four o'clock. Nobody with any sense was up this early. Nobody but mustangs. In the wild, the horses would already be seeking food and water, so they could doze during the hot part of the day.

Sam poured a glass of milk and sipped it. She couldn't force down any of Callie's yogurt. Maybe later.

As she grabbed two horse cookies, Sam wondered if a fourteen-year-old should be fantasizing about hands covered with horse slobber. Right now, she wanted nothing more, because that would mean the Phantom trusted her enough to approach and eat from her hand.

A cricket hushed as she opened the front door. When she reached the end of the garden path, it resumed its chirping.

Both herds had moved much closer to the ranch buildings.

Although smoke lingered in the air, its bitter smell couldn't hide the morning scent of wet grass.

Instead of saddling Ace, Sam slogged through the grass outside the pasture. A flock of dark birds rose in a cloud before her, then coasted out of sight.

The nearest horses raised their heads to watch her approach.

Sam longed to open the gate and walk inside. If only she could just go right up to the stallion and smooth her palm over his sleek shoulder. But she knew better.

Under the best of circumstances, the stallion might flee. And now that she could make him out, Sam knew these were not the best of circumstances.

The Phantom remained apart from the herd. He was ignoring a squealing, teeth-snapping spat between two half-grown colts. Normally the stallion would have reprimanded them. Now, even the lead mare stayed away, too cautious to get near the Phantom.

He'd turned his rippling silver tail to a section of fence. He kicked out one hind hoof, over and over again. He showed no interest in escape and he wasn't kicking hard. The single hoof barely struck the lowest rail.

Sam walked on, hoping he'd notice her without being startled.

His peripheral vision caught Sam's movement when she was still many yards away, and he wheeled away from the fence.

Weeds hung in his heavy mane and grass speckled his hide. His ears flicked forward. Had he heard her coming?

No, the stallion's head tossed in frustration. Curved at the knees, his front legs lifted off the ground, and his anguished neigh put an end to hope.

Chapter Twelve ❧

"Zanzibar," Sam crooned, though the stallion turned and walked away. "Beautiful Zanzibar."

She had to lift his spirits. She took one of the cookies and raised her arm to toss it after the stallion. He'd enjoy it, she thought. Eating was one thing hearing didn't affect, but she'd better make it a hard throw, because he wouldn't hear it fall and some other horse would trot over to gobble it up.

The stallion must have sensed her movement, because he shied right into the cookie. When it struck his flank, he exploded.

The Phantom whirled on the object. Then, like a movie horse attacking a rattlesnake, he trampled the cookie into crumbs and stood panting.

"Oh, my gosh. I'm glad you picked it to be mad at, instead of me," Sam said aloud. The stallion must be full of rage if such a small irritation provoked him into fury.

Then, as if the thought of a small irritation had summoned her, Faith, the blind Medicine Hat filly, wandered into range of the stallion's striking hooves.

"Faith! Get out of there!" Sam shouted. "Go on!"

She flapped her hands toward Faith, trying to spook her away from the stallion. But Faith couldn't see her hands and she cared nothing for her shouts.

"Why do you have to be so stubborn?" Sam called to the filly.

The Phantom seemed equally amazed. Flexing his neck so that his chin bumped his chest, he rumbled, warning her off. Though the other mustangs scattered, the filly kept coming.

Faith's nostrils fluttered as her muzzle skimmed above the ground, searching out the delicious smells of carrots and molasses.

She couldn't be hungry enough to risk injury, so Faith must be reading something in the Phantom's sound or scent that overruled his threats. Sam hoped Faith was right, because what she couldn't see was a rampaging stallion headed right for her.

Sam swallowed hard, remembering that day in the rodeo arena when she'd held her ground against the stallion's charge. Then the Phantom had stopped short of running her down.

This time, the stallion halted so near Faith that the dirt skidding from his front hooves pelted the filly's legs. As if she were offended, not frightened, Faith lifted her hooves—right, left, right—then shook the dust shower off her gold-and-white coat.

The Phantom flattened his ears and darted his head, teeth bared, in her direction. When the filly didn't seem to notice, the Phantom appeared curious rather than upset. He cocked his head. His mane hung in one heavy swathe from the right side of his neck.

Overjoyed, Faith squealed as she found the cookie crumbs. She whuffled her lips over the ground and instinctively turned her tail to the other mustangs, hiding her prize.

"Greedy guts," Sam whispered, and maybe the Phantom made the same comment, because he gave a final snort, then wandered away.

"So, what's happening?"

The male voice at her elbow made Sam turn so fast, she nearly knocked Jake down. When she saw the satisfied grin on his face, she almost wished she had.

"Steady," he said, as if calming a horse.

His hand reached to balance her and she shoved it away.

"Jake! Why do you do that?" Sam demanded.

"Do what?"

"You know what! Sneak up on me. And don't give me that 'aw, shucks, ma'am' shrug," she lectured him.

"Might be I'm just naturally stealthy. Are you insulting my heritage?"

"No," Sam said. She wouldn't give him the satisfaction of arguing over something so silly. Most of the time, she was more interested in Native American traditions than he was. "Just don't expect me to like it when you scare the breath out of me."

Hiding his half smile, Jake turned to watch the horses.

From the corner of her eye, Sam noticed Jake's face was bright red. He never sunburned, so what could be wrong? A question had just reached the tip of her tongue when Sam realized Jake had been standing at the front end of the hose, supporting the nozzle during the fire yesterday. The fire had burned his bronze skin.

He's a tough guy, Sam thought as she considered Jake in his well-washed white T-shirt, faded jeans, boots, and black Stetson. Even after yesterday, which had to have left him bone-tired, he looked ready for a day of work. And it couldn't be six o'clock yet.

"Your horse doin' okay?" he asked. Sam could tell from his tone that he'd heard about the Phantom's deafness.

"No, he's acting really strange. Remember when you broke your leg and spent a month being mad at everyone?"

Jake didn't admit it, but Sam thought his expression showed sympathy for the Phantom.

"And then you ended up cutting off your own cast," Sam reminded him. "I'm sort of worried what *he'll* do when he reaches that stage."

"Jump this wimpy fence," Jake said, rocking it with both hands.

"That's what I'm afraid of," Sam said.

As they watched, the stallion moved among the members of his herd, sniffing each one.

"He's takin' charge," Jake said.

He's trying to, Sam thought. The other horses were still uneasy, though. Their eyes showed white around the edges and their tails lashed nervously. They knew something was wrong.

Faith followed the stallion, but not too closely. She stood under the towering cottonwood, looking up at the creaky branch.

"Someone oughta go up and lop off that branch before it falls and brains somebody," Jake said.

To Sam, the branch didn't look dangerous. "This pasture's huge," she told him. "They'll be okay, don't you think?"

"It goes all the way to the river," Jake acknowledged. "And Dad sprang for new boards so Mrs.

Allen wouldn't have to come home to that damage." Jake nodded toward the broken fence.

"I thought you patched it yesterday," Sam said.

"With scrap lumber. Now we've gotta take it all down and start over."

"So that's why you're here," Sam said, feeling a little disappointed. "I thought maybe my dad sent you over to check on me." When Jake stayed silent, she added, "Can you believe he hasn't been over here once?"

"What's it been, twenty-four hours?" Jake asked.

Sam gave an exasperated sigh. "A kind of important twenty-four hours."

They watched the Phantom's lead mare touch muzzles with Queen.

Had the red dun forgotten that this time last year she'd been the lead mare? Or maybe she didn't hold a grudge, because the mustang mares seemed to be making friends.

Sam thought Jake had forgotten her question about Dad, but then he said, "When I got here yesterday, wasn't Callie sayin' she trusted Queen to take care of herself, even in the fire? Could be Wyatt trusts you, too."

That's what I've been begging Dad to do, Sam thought. *Trust me. Treat me like an adult.*

Sam scratched her head in confusion. It didn't take a psychologist to figure out that now, because

Dad was expecting another child, part of her wanted to be his baby.

"Better go. Quinn's already sheddin' tears big as my fist 'cause he has to help with the fence. He's afraid his friends will leave for the lake without him."

As Jake walked away, his black ponytail, tied with a leather strip, swayed against his white shirt. Sam watched him go.

She guessed there was no one she could discuss this Dad thing with. Not Jake, since he was one of six kids. Not Jen, since she was likely to remain an only child. Gram had said she was "just tickled" to have another chance at grandmothering. And asking Brynna for help just wouldn't be fair. No, Sam decided, this was one thing she'd have to work out on her own.

By midmorning, Sam and Callie had distributed the hay delivered free from Phil's Fill-Up and Feed to all the horses. The girls were pulling pieces of hay from their hair and clothes when a blue car drove into the yard.

Sam had just noticed it was Helen Coley when the phone began ringing inside the house.

"I'll get it," Callie said, so Sam walked out, brushing off her jeans, to greet their visitor.

Helen Coley's short gray hair shone in the morning sun as she climbed out of the Mercedes-Benz, smiling.

Mrs. Coley worked as chauffeur and housekeeper for the Slocums and she was a friend of Gram's.

"Hi Samantha," Mrs. Coley called as she walked around to the car's trunk. "How's that pretty filly of yours doing?"

Mrs. Coley had helped Sam though the crazy days that followed Tempest's birth, while the rest of the Forsters were out on the range for the spring cattle drive.

"Just great," Sam said. "In fact, you just reminded me I miss her."

"Well, I know Trudy must've felt better knowing you were here during the fire," Mrs. Coley said.

Sam buried her hands in her jeans pockets and shrugged her shoulders so high they almost grazed her earlobes.

"Unless Callie's telling her right now," Sam said, glancing toward the house, "she doesn't know yet." Mrs. Coley's eyes widened and Sam made an excuse. "It's just that she's been so concerned about her grandson, I didn't mention it when she called," Sam said.

"Nothing she could do about it from Denver, anyway," Mrs. Coley said, handing Sam a plate with a tall plastic-covered chocolate cake on it. "And it looks like, except for that field over there"—she nodded over the casseroles she was lifting from the trunk—"the ranch came through just fine."

"Yeah," Sam said, but her mouth was actually watering from the cake's aroma, so she had to ask, "What's all this?"

"Didn't Grace call and tell you?" Mrs. Coley tsked her tongue. "Well, I guess she had her hands full over at River Bend, too.

"The church cooking club gets together once a month to bake bread, and we were just doing that when we heard about the fires, so we decided to make a little something for each of the families who got hit by them."

"Great!" Sam said, and as they followed the walk up to Mrs. Allen's front door, Mrs. Coley explained how yesterday's lightning had started spot fires all over the county.

"Luckily no one was hurt," Mrs. Coley said as they managed the door and brought the food inside. "But it does take a chunk out of your day to stop and fight a fire," she chuckled, "so we thought a little help with meals would be welcomed."

"Sorry," Callie said as they walked into the kitchen. "Mrs. Allen called to ask if we had time to take the laundry out of the washing machine and hang it on the clothesline. She was hurrying so to get out of here, she forgot it. And I was just saying good-bye when I heard you trying to get the door open."

"No problem," Mrs. Coley said as she pointed

out what she'd brought. "A macaroni-and-cheese casserole, a broccoli bake, some whole-wheat rolls that just came out of the oven, and a double-fudge layer cake."

Callie's appreciative smile turned brilliant. "You made a meatless dinner. How did you know I was a vegetarian?"

Mrs. Coley tapped her index finger against her lips.

"Where did I hear that?" she mused. "I can't remember, but you know how small towns are. Gossip's a prime form of entertainment."

"Who cares, if I get a dinner like this?" Callie said.

"And this will give us some play time after we hang Mrs. Allen's laundry on the line. The guys are still down there repairing the fence," Sam said.

She and Callie had declared the rest of the day a holiday. They'd spend it outside, reading in the shade of the big cottonwood tree in the pasture, then serenading the horses with songs and Callie's flute.

"Keep an eye on the sky and your radio on, Samantha," Mrs. Coley said as Sam walked her back out to her car.

Sam looked up. The sky had turned gray-blue where it wasn't hidden by clumps of oatmeal-colored clouds.

"In fact, if I were you, I might put that laundry in

the clothes dryer instead of on the line. There's talk of another storm rolling in about sundown, and by the way, the hair on my arms is standing up—I bet it'll be a doozy."

Chapter Thirteen ❧

"Sun dogs are what I'm watching for."

Callie leaned back against the trunk of the old cottonwood tree and peered up through its branches to a patch of sky surrounding the sun.

"Sun dogs," Sam said without glancing up from her book. It was a mystery novel, and she loved to discover clues before the detective.

"You know, those rainbow rings around the sun. Around the moon, too," Callie said. "But those might be called moon dogs."

"What?" Sam said, finally looking at Callie.

"Those hazy rings around the sun are supposed to show moisture and give you a hint that the air's humid," Callie explained. "It's a sign a storm's coming."

Sam held her place in her book with her finger and scooched closer to Callie so that she could see through the same gap between the sand-colored leaves above them.

"If there's lightning, we don't want to be sitting under this tree," Sam said.

She couldn't help remembering the tragedy Gram had recounted from her girlhood. An entire brood mare herd, with their foals, had taken shelter under the only tree in their pasture during an electrical storm. A lightning bolt seeking the quickest path to the earth had struck the tree, then the mares and their foals. All of the horses had been electrocuted.

That was why, according to Gram, River Bend kept only a scattering of trees, none particularly tall, and the barn, fences, and run-in sheds were all made of wood, not metal.

Lightning storms don't happen all that often, Gram had said, *but it only takes one to wipe out an entire saddle herd.*

Or wild herd, Sam thought, looking out at the horses grazing and lazily switching away flies.

Had yesterday's lightning strike increased or decreased the chance that it could happen again today?

"I don't see a sun dog," Sam said when her eyes had gone bleary from squinting at the branch-framed sun.

"That's good, isn't it?" Callie said, but Sam

noticed Callie's eyes had drifted back to her own book. She wasn't really paying attention.

"I guess," Sam said, "but only if it's a foolproof method. Is it?"

"I don't know," Callie said. "But I know this grass sure is prickly."

The girls had put on shorts and sat with their heads and shoulders in the shade and legs extended to catch the sun's warm rays.

"I wouldn't worry so much about lightning if Mrs. Allen's pasture had more trees. I mean, why is there only one tall tree in the entire pasture?"

"Sam!" Callie said in frustration.

"Sorry. Go ahead, I won't interrupt your reading anymore. I hate it when someone does it to me."

"It's not that. It's Mrs. Allen's pasture. There are hundreds of fenced acres for the sanctuary. It runs down to the river and partway to the mountains. There are gullies and hills and scrub and trees of all sizes. We can only see this one tree, but when the storm blew in yesterday, you didn't see the mustangs standing around going, 'Yep, let's go stand under that tree,' did you?"

Sam searched her mind and decided the Phantom's herd had probably been fleeing from high ground, down to a lower spot, yesterday. They just hadn't figured on the low spot being damp and, probably, that had attracted the lightning.

"Yeah, I bet you're right," Sam said, nodding.

"And wild horses, especially, would know what to do."

"You'd think," Callie said, taking off her glasses to rub the bridge of her nose.

They both leaned back against the tree, feeling more relaxed.

Sam had closed her eyes, thinking she might nap, when suddenly her knees felt cool. The sun must have gone behind a cloud, she thought drowsily.

"Sam."

Had she really heard Callie's voice?

"Don't move."

Was there a bumblebee crawling on her shirt or a butterfly perched on her book? Sam yawned and opened her eyes.

The first thing she noticed was that the coolness on her knees was caused by a shadow. The shadow was cast by a horse. She almost stopped breathing when she saw that horse was the Phantom.

Head lowered, the silver stallion sniffed at her sneakers, checking her out just as he had the members of his herd. It was the first time since the fire that she'd seen him this close. The burn on his neck looked no worse than yesterday. In fact, it seemed a little smaller to her, but maybe she was just hoping.

His brown eyes showed through his heavy forelock, and they rolled toward Callie, checking to see if she was a threat. Hooves planted, unwilling to move any closer, he rocked forward so that his breath warmed Sam's ankles.

His muscles trembled. He wanted to come nearer, but he'd already broken the rules of flight distance to see if it was really her.

His ears cupped forward, waiting for his secret name.

Zanzibar, you can't hear me, she thought, heart aching for the magnificent stallion, *so it won't matter if I just talk to you in my mind. Heal soon, good boy.*

Just then, a bird coasted down from the cottonwood tree and startled the stallion.

"Oh Sam, I'm so sorry," Callie said as the stallion galloped away. "If I hadn't been here, you could have touched him."

"I don't think so. He was pretty spooky."

"I'm going to go back to the house to get my flute. While I'm gone, you can give it another try. I've read that horses have phenomenal receptors in their skins, so you really should try to lay your hands on him, and let him know you're with him, though he can't hear that secret name."

"Okay," Sam said.

"Really. I bet you've heard people say some performance horse—you know, a champion cutting horse or top-ranked dressage horse—was psychic. They're not, though. They just feel the rider's signal before she thinks she's given one."

Callie rose slowly to her feet and walked away before Sam could say anything, but the stallion didn't return.

Sunset had claimed the sky before Callie came back. She'd traded her shorts for a gauzy lavender skirt. In one hand she held her glittering silver flute. In the other, she carried a basket filled with dandelions.

"I wish I had chamomile oil," Callie said as she settled beside Sam.

Bewildered by Callie's wish, Sam just stared at her. Maybe Brynna had a point when she talked about Callie's mumbo jumbo. Or was it hocus-pocus?

"What are you talking about?" Sam asked. "Like for chamomile tea?"

"No, for aromatherapy," Callie explained. "It's supposed to ease sadness, and I think it could help the Phantom."

"Well, he hasn't come near enough to smell anything," Sam said. "So what's with the dandelions? Will they do something?"

Even though she was skeptical, Sam was willing to try anything for her horse.

"Do something?" Callie asked. "Yeah, we're going to weave them into garlands like this"—Callie used her thumbnail to cut a hole in one dandelion stem, slid a second stem through it, and repeated the process until she had a chain of four—"and make ourselves crowns of flowers, to wear while we sing to the horses."

"So they don't have any magical powers or anything?" Sam asked, taking a handful of the dandelions Callie had picked.

"Magical powers? What are *you* talking about?" Callie asked.

"Never mind," Sam said. Smiling, she set to work making a garland of flowers for her auburn hair.

Queen was the first horse charmed by the music.

Callie played a medieval tune that wafted over the pasture, sounding haunting and familiar. Queen took long loping steps from across the grass and stopped just a few yards away.

Sam couldn't sing along because she didn't know the words, but she hummed, and soon Queen had been joined by the honey-brown mare and Licorice, Windfall, and Roman.

"Gotta breathe," Callie gasped quietly, lips parting from the flute.

"Play something I can sing," Sam urged her. Then, sheepishly, she said, "The Phantom likes my voice, and I promise to shoo off any coyotes I attract."

Callie frowned a little, but then she began playing one of Sam's favorite songs.

The high notes of the flute soared sweeter than Sam's voice, but she sang "Greensleeves" until her throat hurt.

"Alas my love you do me wrong to cast me off so discourteously, when I have lov'd you so long, delighting in your company."

It was stupid to sing yourself to tears, but Sam couldn't help it.

When Callie stopped, flexing her fingers, the poignant notes lingered on the evening breeze and Sam counted eight horses, side by side. They didn't graze or nip at each other; they just listened. Only their manes and tails drifted, all to one side, and behind them, Sam could see the Phantom.

"Is he standing in the second row because he can't hear and just wants to know why they're here? Or do you think you're right, that he can feel the vibrations?"

"Who cares?" Callie said. "He's here, not moping around kicking the fence."

Sam grinned. Callie was right.

When Callie began playing something that sounded like an Irish jig, it matched Sam's mood. Her spirits rose and circled the Nevada sky until Roman, for no reason Sam could discern, wheeled on the Phantom.

The silver stallion didn't back down, but he was obviously surprised.

Mustangs scattered away from the flashing teeth and hooves thudding on ribs. Faith reared, crying out as if she'd break up the battle, but the two males ignored her.

Sam jumped to her feet. "What's going on?"

"He's not even a stallion, is he?" Callie asked, confused.

"He's a jerk!" Sam shouted, but when she stepped forward, hands waving, the Phantom looked her way and received a wrenching bite on the neck from the gelding.

"Don't distract him," Callie said, grabbing Sam's arm, but it was too late.

The Phantom squealed in pain and frustration, gave a final kick that struck only the air, and then ran.

The thunder of his hoofbeats matched the sudden rumbling in the clouds overhead. The Phantom was gone.

Chapter Fourteen ↷

The storm didn't break that night. Or the next morning.

And the Phantom had vanished.

Because he was gone, Sam talked herself into doing more work for Mrs. Allen. After the paint explosion, Sam had figured she was done with the fence until Mrs. Allen returned and bought more, but when she'd forced herself to look in the barn where the first few cans had been, she found even more.

It had been awkward, carrying all the gear out to the fence on horseback. But Ace had proven himself the perfect, unflappable ranch horse again.

While he grazed a few yards off, Sam stood at the

new section of fence the Elys had built, painting it to match the rest.

That's what I *look* like I'm doing, Sam thought.

In fact, she was hoping Dr. Scott would just drive up and give her tons of advice on how to help the Phantom.

"Not gonna happen," Sam told herself.

Dr. Scott had a busy practice among horse owners in Darton, as well as local ranchers. If he had anything to tell her, he'd call, not drive out to Deerpath Ranch.

Besides, Pirate needed any extra time the vet could spare.

The fancy-marked bay colt had stolen Sam's heart the first time she'd seen him. If he survived the physical and emotional trauma from this accident, Dr. Scott would deserve all the credit.

Maybe she could convince him to adopt the colt!

Yeah, Sam thought as she swished the paintbrush around in the thick red paint.

"Ace, wouldn't that be perfect?" She looked over her shoulder at the bay gelding and was surprised to see he was staring past her.

Sam whirled. Could Ace have spotted the Phantom?

But she didn't see him. No matter how long she stared, he simply wasn't there.

She had to keep painting. She had to fight the

desire to saddle Ace and search for the stallion, because she wouldn't find a wild mustang who didn't want to be found.

He'd come to her when he was ready, just as he had yesterday, when she'd been sitting under the cottonwood tree.

The Phantom would be fine without her.

Wild things took care of themselves.

She'd learned that lesson before, but she kept forgetting, or thinking she knew best. Most of the time, the Phantom didn't need her help at all.

When Sam rode Ace back to Deerpath Ranch for lunch, she discovered Callie had taken down all of Mrs. Allen's curtains.

Sunlight flooded the house, revealing Persian carpets in brilliant jewel tones—emerald green, ruby red, sapphire blue.

"I never even noticed there were rugs in here," Sam said.

"Aren't they cool? I love this!" Callie said. Her fuchsia hair was covered with a kerchief and her glasses were nearly opaque with dust.

"You love doing housework?" Sam asked. She felt her eyebrows disappearing under her bangs.

"I like revealing stuff," Callie explained. "I think that's part of what I like about doing hair. You can take someone with just one good feature, and by arranging their hair right, make them look beautiful."

"Don't look at me like that," Sam said, holding her hands before her face.

"Like what?" Callie said, but she didn't stop.

"Like you're searching for my one good feature," she said, raising her voice as Callie protested.

Then Sam thought of something more important.

"Dr. Scott hasn't called, has he? He promised he would."

"No, but hey, Mrs. Allen called again," Callie said from the laundry room, as she tugged wet curtains out of the washing machine.

"What did she have to say?"

"She said Gabe was a little better, but he's all wrapped up in worrying."

"Gosh, I would be, too," Sam said.

"She said he's worried about his summer school class, his friends who were in the accident, what the kids who weren't in the accident are saying about him. . . ."

An unexpected vision of a hospital room—white, crammed with monitors and anxious faces—replaced the sunny ranch kitchen. She'd been in a room like that for days, following her accident.

Of course Gabe was worried, now that he was conscious. There wasn't much else to do.

As clearly as if she'd been there yesterday, Sam saw that white room with crayon drawings taped up on one wall. She couldn't remember who'd sent them to cheer her up, but she remembered Dad's anguished face buried in his brown, scarred cowboy's hands.

". . . building up to something," Callie was saying pointedly.

"What?" Sam said, jerked out of her memory. She filled her glass with water, cranked the faucet off, and focused on Callie, standing framed in the laundry room doorway.

"I said," Callie repeated, "I can tell from her voice that Mrs. Allen is building up to something."

"Like what?" Sam sipped the water.

"Bringing him here to stay, maybe," Callie mused.

"No way. Not until he's totally out of danger," Sam said, dismissing the idea. "Emergency medical care out here hasn't improved that much since my accident. It's too risky. The power goes out and the phones don't always work."

Was she replaying some mental tape of Dad's voice, trying to explain why she had to move to San Francisco?

"We're not on Mars," Callie said, with a faint scolding in her voice. "Darton has Angel Flight rescue helicopters."

"Whatever," Sam said abruptly.

It had taken months to build up her nerve for riding. She didn't want to think of that hospital anymore.

Callie shrugged and Sam knew she should go help Callie fold the unwieldy curtains, but she felt lightheaded.

Worse, thoughts of the hospital had kindled a new idea. Could the Phantom feel the way she had? Knowing he was someplace safe, but hating it?

Sam gathered a jar of peanut butter, bread, and a knife, then started searching for jam. Oh, good, Mrs. Allen had blackberry jam, homemade by the look of the label. Sam set to work building a sandwich.

Then, just so the awkward silence with Callie wouldn't spin out too long, she asked, "Did you tell her about the fire?"

"Uh-huh," Callie said.

"What?" Sam dropped the messy knife and walked in to face Callie.

"I told her there was a lightning strike, a brush fire that scorched a few acres of her property and the only thing that burned was a piece of fence that the Elys fixed, and you were painting."

"What did she say?" Sam asked, but she could guess. Callie's explanation didn't make the fire a catastrophe. It sounded like they'd been lucky.

"She congratulated us on handling things, and said a little vacation over at your house would probably do Imp and Angel some good."

"I don't know," Sam said as she returned to the kitchen and picked up the peanut butter knife, which had landed on the cutting board. "The cowboys will treat them like dogs, not royalty."

As Sam finished making her sandwich, she wondered if Callie's positive attitude got the credit for making so many things turn out right.

Sam was just ready to bite into her sandwich when Dr. Scott called.

"Sam, I'm sorry I haven't been more help to you girls, over there alone . . ." he began.

As usual, the young vet sounded so busy and concerned, Sam felt sorry for him.

"No big deal," she said. "If anything had gone wrong, we would have called you. Except for that burn on the Phantom's neck, the mustangs seem fine."

"Good. That's what I wanted to hear. What about the Boston bulls?" he asked.

Startled, Sam said, "Imp and Angel? They were fine last time I saw them. They're over at River Bend. Why, was something wrong? Were you treating them for something?"

Sam rubbed her forehead. If Mrs. Allen had forgotten wet laundry, she could have forgotten a list of pills they were supposed to give the dogs. So much for keeping a positive—

"No, I'm not treating them for anything. There's no cure for being spoiled rotten," he joked. "I just wondered if they'd developed worse-than-usual sniffles. Dogs with their facial structure—pugs and boxers, for instance—can have sinus problems, and I was just thinking—huh." He ended the sentence with a grunt of surprise, but seemed willing to drop the subject. "I'm glad they're doing well."

The silence that followed made Sam uneasy. Dr. Scott hadn't mentioned Pirate. For the first time, she realized his injuries could have been fatal.

"The bay colt," Dr. Scott said slowly, "is still hanging in there."

"How badly was he hurt?" Sam managed.

"Real bad," Dr. Scott said bluntly. "Definitely traumatized, but I'm not questioning our decision to save him."

Sam ached for Pirate. Dr. Scott's words told her he *had* questioned the choice. When he went on to list Pirate's first- and second-degree burns, complications from smoke inhalation, and his refusal to eat, Sam wondered, too.

But could she have let him die? No.

"He's a beautiful colt, and smart," Sam told Dr. Scott. "He's worth saving."

"I know. And he's a fighter. He'll make it," the vet said. His heavy sigh made Sam wonder how much sleep he'd gotten since taking in the colt. "But I don't think he's ever going back on the range, Sam, and somebody's going to have to do some major work to make him a happy horse."

Maybe you? Sam thought, crossing her fingers as the vet went on.

"Even though I've kept him pretty sedated so I can work on him, he's confused and . . . I wouldn't trust his lungs to function through a winter on the range. A severe dust storm would be bad, too. Shoot, just running from predators might be too much for him." The vet was quiet for a minute and Sam heard what sounded like a pencil tapping on a desk. "It sorta comes down to 'what price freedom,' y'know?"

What price freedom?

Sam had never heard the expression, but she knew instinctively what it meant. Was freedom worth dying for?

"I think you'll bring him around, Dr. Scott. You did it for the Phantom, and you're a really good vet. Everyone says so."

"They do? Well, that's good to know." His tone was grateful and somehow lighter. "Thanks, Sam. Ever since I watched how that buckskin of yours improved, I knew I could count on you."

Rain and rumbling thunder came in the afternoon, and the wild horses scattered.

Standing in the barn with her arm draped around Ace's neck, Sam stared through the gray curtain of rain, hoping the mustangs had sought the sheltered gulches farther out in the pasture.

When lightning crackled overhead, Sam held her breath, but no explosion brightened the sky or shook the ground.

Where was the Phantom? Did he see the lightning and remember the storm that had taken his hearing? Was he afraid?

With a snort, Ace shifted his weight and leaned

against Sam as if she were another horse.

"Hey, boy, is the sound of the rain making you sleepy?"

The hissing downpour didn't last long. Soon Sam could hear single drops pelting a tin roof.

"The storm's moving on," Sam told Ace, and at first, when he straightened and tossed his head, she thought he was responding to her weather prediction.

Then Ace's ears pointed at the pasture. A silent neigh shook through him and his eyes fixed on something Sam could not see.

"What is it, Ace?" Sam's pulse pounded in her throat. She stared until her eyes burned, but the muddy pasture remained empty.

There! Just as lightning glimmered inside a far-off cloud bank, she saw a pale form. Without Ace's trembling attention, she would have dismissed it as wishful thinking, because the ghostly beast with floating mane and tail might have been ripped from the clouds and formed into a horse by her imagination.

Drawn like a sleepwalker into the departing rain, Sam left the barn and headed toward the pasture.

She blinked the raindrops from her eyelashes. It was him. Every cell in her body recognized him.

Racing and rearing, soundless as a spirit horse raging in a nightmare, the Phantom rose on his hind legs, hooves reaching for the sky, as if he were fighting back.

Water splashed behind Sam. Tires splattered through puddles and Sam turned to see Dad's truck driving toward her.

She searched for one last glimpse of the stallion, but he was gone.

Sam walked toward Dad's truck, pushing her dripping bangs back from her eyes.

"Hey there. I hear you're the boss of this outfit," Dad joked.

Sam smiled. Someday, she *would* be the boss of an entire ranch.

Dad's eyes swept over her sodden hair and clothes, telling her she could have used a hat and slicker like he did, but he didn't say it.

Then Imp and Angel jumped from the truck cab, landed in the mud, gave their coats a quick shake, and ran in barking ecstasy for the house.

"Guess they're glad to be home," Dad said. "Pesky little critters. They're not fit to be in the house with a cat, that's for sure. Truth is, though, I think Dallas was getting to like them."

"Dallas?"

"Yeah, I couldn't help noticing that all the time he was calling them overgrown rats and saying they were good for nothing but fishin' bait, he was feeding them dinner scraps and scratching behind their ears."

Sam laughed, then made a pretense of going out to check the bolts on the pasture gate. She hoped that would explain why she was standing out in the rain.

"Good job," Dad said. "We need to change some of our latches, or make sure they're shut, because we've had too many loose horses over the last year or so."

Sam winced. It didn't look like a coincidence that she'd been there both times Dark Sunshine had escaped.

Dad shook his head at her guilty expression.

"Not sayin' any of it's your fault. In fact, I'm darn proud of you, honey. Especially with what you're doin' over here. I've managed to stay away and let you run the show, but your Gram's been askin' around."

Maybe it had been Gram, Sam thought, but Dad was rubbing the back of his neck. He always did that when he was uncomfortable.

Who had checked up on her? Mrs. Coley, when she brought dinner? Jake, when he came to mend the fence? Dr. Scott, when he gave her an update on Pirate?

Dad wouldn't have done the snooping himself, but she'd bet he'd urged Gram to get on the phone and talk with all of them.

"You didn't have to stay away," Sam said.

Dad bumped his Stetson back from eyes that widened in surprise.

"No ma'am, I didn't, but you've been asking me to trust you. Now seemed like a good time to stand up and do it."

Sam's tongue wet her lips. She didn't know what

to say. Dad sounded like he'd had to fight himself not to run over here.

Maybe he hadn't stayed away because he didn't care. Maybe he wasn't preoccupied with the coming baby.

"Thanks, I guess," she said.

"Here's the thing, honey. Right now, I need to know where you are, every breathin' minute, day and night. So, what am I gonna do when you go out on dates? And off to college? Shoot, I can hardly stand thinkin' about the kind of fool trouble kids get in."

Dad rubbed the back of his neck again and Sam smiled. That speech had been world-class long for Dad, and there was nothing left to do but hug him for it.

So she did.

It was ten o'clock at night. Callie had gone to bed, but Sam had finished her mystery and was restlessly searching Mrs. Allen's shelves for something else to read.

She sat on the couch, flipping through an art history book. It sure didn't have much of a plot. She closed it carefully.

She'd already had two slices of chocolate cake, so a snack was out.

She should go to bed, because she was determined to make major progress on painting the fence tomorrow.

Suddenly the phone rang. It couldn't be good news this late, but Sam snatched up the receiver before the phone could ring again and wake Callie.

"Samantha? It doesn't sound as if I've awakened you."

"No, you haven't, Mrs. Allen. What time is it there?"

"Midnight or thereabouts, but I have someone who wants to talk with you."

Sam reeled with misgivings. It could only be Mrs. Allen's grandson, Gabe. She didn't even know him.

Sam folded her legs up on the couch beside her, wishing she could gather her thoughts so efficiently.

Callie had sensed Mrs. Allen was building up to something. Was this it?

Sam wished Callie had answered the phone. She could handle anything.

Maybe Gabe was just bored, Sam thought as the sound of rustling, which might have been bedsheets, came over the line.

Yeah, boredom. The confinement might be driving Gabe nuts. He had been an active kid. . . .

Had been. Oh good, Sam.

And then he was talking.

"Hi. This is Gabe. My grandmother said I should call."

The male voice sounded normal. Not as deep as Jake's, but surprisingly — Sam searched for a word — breezy, she guessed, for a kid in his position. His grandmother had told him to call and, bored, he'd given in.

She could handle small talk, couldn't she?

"What's up?" she asked.

"Not me," he said with a bitter laugh.

Sam curled in on herself as if he'd punched her in the stomach.

How stupid could she be? What an idiot thing to say! But, wow, the kid had some guts, trying to joke when, unless something wonderful had happened, he couldn't even move his legs.

"So, what year are you in school?" Sam asked. That would be safe. If Mrs. Allen was counting on her to cheer Gabe up, she'd fall back on the most ordinary of questions.

"I'll be a junior."

"One year ahead of me," Sam said.

She drew a deep breath. Now what?

"Look, this was a dumb idea," Gabe said.

"No! Are you kidding?" Sam said quickly. "I was sitting here bored out of my mind. When you come visit your grandma, bring something fun to read, will you?"

"That might be a while," he said.

"That's okay." She stared at the ceiling. A faint crack zigzagged through the plaster. She was following it with her eyes when she said, "I got locked up in the hospital a couple of years ago."

"Yeah?"

"I fell off my horse and managed to put my head where his hooves were."

"Ouch."

"Naw, I don't remember a thing. About that part."

"I hate this place," he said.

Sam heard voices in the background. Was his mother there, as well as Mrs. Allen? Maybe none of them could sleep.

"Yeah, I was unconscious for a while, so I wasn't awake to hate it, much."

"Like a coma?" he asked, bluntly. "You're supposed to be cheering me up."

"Hey, you called me," Sam blurted.

They both laughed, then, but she added, "Yeah, like a coma."

"You musta hated that horse."

"It wasn't his fault, and besides . . ."

All at once, Sam found herself telling Gabe about her time in San Francisco and Blackie's flight into the wilderness. When Gabe prodded her for details, she explained the controversy over the West's wild horses, told him about the Phantom's herd, and finally told him about the explosion that had robbed him of his hearing.

When she got to that part, she stopped. Gabe had been quiet for a long time. Had she babbled him to sleep?

This *was* dumb.

Gabe had been right twenty minutes ago when

he'd said that. Why was she spilling her life story, and the Phantom's, to a stranger?

"So what are they gonna do with him?" he said finally.

"I don't know. My stepmother is the manager of the BLM's wild horse program here, and she says— well, it's really sappy—she says since I'm the best friend he has, I get to make the decision."

"That is sappy," Gabe agreed. "Why you? He's the wild horse. Let him decide."

Irritation flashed through Sam.

"Easy for you to say," she told him.

But then she wondered if Gabe was really talking about the Phantom. Maybe he felt like all his choices had been taken away from him.

"Yeah." His voice sounded a little fainter. Had he shifted positions, or was she tiring him out? Wasn't Mrs. Allen there to tell him to get off the phone and go to sleep?

At last, he said, "Tell me what the Phantom looks like."

"He's the most beautiful horse in the world. He's silver gray, but sometimes, like in moonlight or bright sun, he looks pure white. And . . ." Sam felt her throat close. "Most of all, he's wild. And, even though he's really confused right now, by not being able to hear . . ." Sam cleared her throat, trying not to cry. "I can still see it in his eyes. In racehorses, they call it 'the look of eagles,' have you ever heard that?" Sam heard something on the other end of the line. Maybe he'd transferred the receiver to his other ear, but she couldn't stop talking. "Well, the Phantom's got that look and that spirit and that's why I won't adopt him. I will never, ever take that away from him—"

"Samantha?" It was Mrs. Allen's voice, kind but impatient. "Thank you, so much," she whispered. "He's just been so nervous and didn't want to talk with any of his friends here. You did a great job of making him get sleepy. Nighty-night."

Sam hung up the phone, but she didn't go to bed for a long, lonely hour.

Chapter Fifteen ∂

Sam yawned as she looked back over the sections of painted fence.

She'd been feeling so lazy, she'd ridden out bare-back this morning.

Ace was ground-tied back where she'd started this morning, and the distance to him seemed to stretch for a mile. As if he felt her gaze, the gelding lifted his red-brown head and tossed his forelock back from his eyes. When he saw she had nothing interesting in mind, he dropped to his knees, then flopped to one side and rolled, enjoying the luxury of rubbing his hide on the short, damp grass.

Beyond Ace, Sam could see Callie leading Queen.

The red dun mare had been standing at the fence

this morning, waiting as if her time with the wild ones was finished, so Callie had decided to lead her on a walk around Deerpath Ranch. Following Sam's directions, they were going in search of the hot spring.

Everyone was enjoying a peaceful and contented morning, except her. She was still working on the fence.

Sam knew she was making progress, but the old weathered wood seemed to soak up the paint as soon as she brushed it on.

She was lucky Mrs. Allen only wanted the part facing the road painted. It would take a professional with a sprayer, according to Brynna, to paint the whole thing.

In a way, Sam was glad the fence ran on forever. If the pasture hadn't looked like endless acres, the Phantom's herd would have been frantic to escape. She'd seen horses fresh off the range come into the corrals at Willow Springs.

They flung themselves at the fences, trying to jump metal rails they had no hope of clearing.

Should the Phantom be captive or free?

She tried not to think about her conversation with Gabe.

Let him decide, he'd told her.

Sure, and did he let his cat decide it wanted to go outside and run across the freeway? Did he let his dog decide when it wanted to go to the vet for vaccinations? What did some guy in Colorado know about mustangs?

Sam slapped her paintbrush down so hard that reddish spots splattered her legs.

The Phantom had had such spots after the explosion. They were gone now. He'd seen to that by rolling in the grass, or maybe he'd gone down to the river.

The river. Maybe . . .

Hotspot nickered for attention.

Behind her, Ace's hooves moved closer, but Hotspot seemed more interested in human companionship.

"Hey, girl," Sam said. "Are you lonesome?"

All morning, the Appaloosa mare had followed along on the other side of the fence. Since Roman's attack on the Phantom, the two herds had split, and Hotspot wandered between them, an outsider to both bands.

"Do you want to go home, girl?" Sam asked.

The mare watched with eyes that almost matched her chocolate-brown face.

"Do you miss your baby?"

Hotspot shook her head so hard that her mane flipped from one side of her neck to the other.

"Well, that's not very nice, so I'm going to assume a fly was buzzing around your head and I just couldn't see it."

Sam didn't tell Hotspot that her colt, Shy Boots,

had been matched with a nursemaid burro in her absence, or that Brynna had said Hotspot would be going home.

By law, Brynna had to notify Linc Slocum in a timely manner that his horse had been found running with a wild band.

When Sam had asked how long a "timely manner" was, Brynna had mused a minute.

"Well," she'd said, at last. "It's too late for Hotspot to resume nursing her foal. Her milk's dried up and Shy Boots has bonded with the jenny. So I think a timely manner will be after things are resolved with the Phantom.

"I don't want Linc Slocum coming down here with a trailer while we have a wild herd all rounded up. The less that man is around mustangs, the better, as far as I'm concerned." Then Brynna's voice had taken on a dreamy tone. "And you know, I could charge him a trespass fee for letting her eat on the public lands. Wouldn't that be fun?"

"Do it!" Sam had cheered. When Brynna let herself be a friend instead of a stepmother, Sam loved it.

"I'm thinking about it," Brynna said. Then she cleared her throat. "I try to be a good neighbor, but that man tempts me to give him what he deserves."

Suddenly, Ace's snort and the clack of a hoof on rock drew Sam's eyes away from her painting.

Faith and the Phantom came across the pasture together.

The silver stallion and the half-grown filly had become buddies.

At first Sam had been a little sad, thinking the Phantom gave the filly eyes and she acted as his ears. As she watched the two, though, she realized they were just friends. Faith constantly sniffed and snuffled the stallion, as if he were a fascinating addition to her world, and the Phantom tolerated the filly's sassy refusal to be afraid of him.

Just now, Faith moved away from the stallion. She left him to his skittish, watchful walk while she meandered over to eat a few shoots of grass growing beneath her favorite tree.

Sam had been squatting to paint a bottom fence rail. Now she stood slowly to get a better look at her horse.

The Phantom's coat shone white in the summer sun. He must have given himself a dust bath, because not only were the red spots gone, but so was the mud on his coat and the clumps of dirt in his streaming silver tail.

He jolted into a nervous trot as if something spurred him. He didn't look confused and bewildered, but instead surprised.

Sam held her breath, not daring to hope.

The stallion burst into a lope. Long, fluid strides took him sweeping just yards away from the fence. Ace neighed and the stallion snorted, then snorted again as he kept moving.

Sam recognized the snort. It wasn't a greeting. It meant, "What's this?" He didn't slow, but his gait shifted to a speedy trot. Something had his attention, but what?

He stopped, ears pricked after Faith.

No big deal, Sam told herself. He's been doing that all along. He's never stopped trying to hear.

Then, his left ear swiveled toward the tree and his chin lifted.

That was different.

Suddenly, in the same second, three things happened.

Faith's Medicine Hat head jerked up from grazing. The cottonwood branch gave a final snap. And the Phantom bolted toward the tree.

Thick as Sam's arm and covered with fluttering leaves, the branch fell to the ground. It didn't hit Faith, or the stallion. After a minute of sniffing muzzles and circling, the horses moved away.

Be calm, Sam told herself, but an argument ping-ponged back and forth inside her mind.

The Phantom could have been reacting to Faith's movement with his eyes, not his ears.

But his left ear had already been listening to something up in that tree.

It wasn't like he'd rescued the blind filly. She'd rescued herself.

But he *had* bolted toward the sound. Why? Horses assumed every strange movement was a threat, didn't they? Except that herd stallions had a job to do, and that job included protecting younger, weaker members of their herds.

Suddenly, Sam knew what *she* had to do.

It was two miles to the La Charla drop-off and the gate on the other side of the river. Two miles was a long walk, but it wasn't bad on horseback, and instinct told her the Phantom would be more likely to follow Ace than her alone.

Sam remembered the time the Phantom and Ace had run side by side, taking her to the stallion's valley, and the time he'd matched strides with Ace as the gelding galloped through the Thread the Needle pass above Willow Springs, leading the stallion home.

"What do you think, boy?" Sam whispered to the gelding.

Ace lifted his head and one of his split reins dangled within reach. Sam grabbed it. With slow, quiet steps, she led him back to a gate and through it.

Holding her breath, Sam vaulted up onto Ace's bare back. Her fingers fumbled with reins and mane. So much depended on this. She had to do everything right.

With the faintest tightening of her legs, she urged Ace forward. Sam pretended to ignore the other horses as he began walking.

Two miles was long enough to snag the Phantom's attention. If she'd guessed right, he would be curious enough to follow. If he followed, and his honey-brown mare came after him, the rest of the band would fall into step.

She hoped.

Thudding hooves and a squeal made Ace tense beneath her. Sam looked back in time to see Roman and the Phantom confront each other again. In a single glance, the gelding took in the commanding lift of the Phantom's head and the challenge ended.

Tail swishing, Roman returned to grazing.

Celebration started in Sam's heart, but she kept Ace walking toward the river.

The smell of the fire lingered, but it was different. The scent wasn't a bitter reminder of destruction. It had grown faint, turning to an almost cozy smell, like a barbecue or campfire, and even that faded as they approached the river.

Ace pulled at the reins and his hooves danced impatiently. He wanted to swing into a jog or turn and mingle with the horses behind them.

Sam listened hard, trying to figure out how many horses followed, but the La Charla rushed with the chitchat sound that had earned the river its name, obscuring all but the loudest hoofbeats.

Sam didn't turn to glance over her shoulder. Wasn't there some story about a woman who looked back and then turned to stone? Her penalty for looking back would be harsh, too. If she made even one of them shy, it could ruin everything. Today, she could be patient.

When they reached the drop-off, the lush scent of water-loving willow trees crowded out the last wisp of smoke.

Sam could hear the sound of the river rolling over rocks even before she reached the edge. And then there was a swoop of wings above as a swallow slanted past her, dropping down through the air to hover over the silver rills.

A huff of breath told her the stallion followed closely, but she kept her legs tight against Ace's sides, urging him to navigate the path before the stallion caught up.

When she'd ridden out here with Brynna, she'd noticed it was just wide enough for a single horse.

Bareback on Ace, there was no way she wanted to share that trail with the Phantom, especially if the stallion was in a hurry to reach the river.

"You can lead a horse to water but you can't make him drink," Gram said sometimes, and though Sam wasn't exactly sure what she meant, the saying came back to her now.

She could see the gate on the other side of the river. She'd led the Phantom to freedom. She couldn't make him choose it, but she could sure open the gate.

As soon as they reached the sandy riverbank, Ace gave a sharp jerk against the bit. He might really be thirsty.

As soon as Sam slipped from his back, he lowered his head to drink.

Don't look back, Sam told herself once more, then took a giant step into the river.

She managed not to screech at the slap of snowmelt on her knees and thighs.

It's hot. It feels good, she thought as she kept walking.

She tried to see through the reflective surface of the water, but she couldn't. Her sneakered feet would have to find a way between the rocks. She really didn't want to fall. The splashing commotion could still send the horses running.

Almost there. She could see the gate was wide enough to drive a truck through. And the latch was just a loop of wire settled over a straight post. Piece of cake. It would take her about two seconds to open it.

Then it was up to the Phantom.

When a submerged branch snagged the hem of her cutoffs, she worked it loose and kept slogging, with cold-numbed legs, through the water.

At last! The shallows fell to her knees, her calves—her legs prickled with goose bumps that almost hurt—then the water was at her ankles, and she was out!

She lifted the loop of twisted wire and shoved the gate with her shoulder. It swung open.

"Good, good, good," she muttered, and propped the gate open with a rock.

Only then did she look back.

The Phantom stood in the shallows, a few yards upstream from Ace, drinking. Blue shadows cast by the willows and water showed every curve of muscle below his silver hide. His lips touched the river, but his eyes stared across the surface of the water, watching her return.

Sam tried to keep her steps slow. Although the Phantom had come down the trail to the river, his herd stayed up above, milling and watching as they always did when their leader guided them to water.

Maybe the days she'd spent at the fence since the fire made her familiar to him, because the stallion met her while she was still knee-deep in the river.

Had he always seemed this big? A white wall of a horse, with his sweet leathery smell, he whuffled his lips over her shirt, then tickled her neck with his whiskers. He stood so near, she couldn't see his ears when she whispered to him.

"Zanzibar," Sam said, daring to curve one arm around his neck. "Are you all right, boy?"

The stallion lowered his head, rubbed his forelock against her chest and, before Sam could steady herself, rammed her into the river.

She hit the river bottom on the seat of her cutoffs. Her head went under and she came up sputtering.

She ducked as the stallion gave a buck of sheer high spirit. Those hooves could hurt, but . . .

"No, boy," she cautioned him as his shoulder hit

hers, sending her back into the river once more.

"Some game," she sputtered, spitting out a mouthful of water. "This stuff is full of bact—"

The stallion stopped. He turned his left ear her way. Then he shook his thick mane. His hindquarters gathered and smooth muscles bunched beneath his silken hide to launch him back up the path to his herd.

An imperious neigh warned Sam to *move*, but the order wasn't for her. It was for the honey-brown mare who jumped from the lip of the drop-off down to the middle of the path, followed by the nipping, kicking, bumping mustangs on her heels.

Sam splashed ashore, sprinted toward Ace, grabbed his reins, and flattened herself against a boulder. For a minute, it was raining horses and rocks and river water. Tons of hot hide and horseflesh surrounded her as they crashed into the water, making waves and waterfalls of white foam.

After days of captivity, they headed for the open gate on the wild side of the river.

Ace's longing neigh rang out as the lead mare reached the far shore.

Now the Phantom scrabbled back down the trail and waded into the river.

All the commotion was on the other side now. The stallion found a deep place in the river and swam.

His mane floated on the river and long liquid ripples spread from his chest as he crossed.

Even when he'd reached the other side, he never looked back—not for her, not for Ace or for Faith, who stood neighing on the bank.

The Phantom had chosen freedom.

From
Phantom Stallion
↩ 17 ↪
MOUNTAIN MARE

The trail out of camp grew steep in a hurry, but it was easy to follow as it cut through the changing vegetation. In minutes, Sam and Jen were riding beside a mountain's rock face. As the horses climbed higher, the air turned crisp and sweet as stream water.

The trail was wide enough that the girls could have ridden side by side, but they didn't. Because he was calmer, Ace led while Silly followed a few horse lengths behind.

With only rock on her right, Sam noticed the plants clustered on the hillside to her left. Dust covered the leaves of some plant she didn't recognize.

Stones clattered and brush cracked up ahead.

"Deer?" Sam asked, glancing over her shoulder at Jen.

"Probably," Jen answered. "I don't think we're high enough for mountain sheep and if it was a cougar, we wouldn't hear it."

"That's comforting," Sam said. Her tone was sarcastic, but her scalp tightened and chills rained down her neck as she checked the rock wall, too.

"Sorry," Jen apologized, wincing.

It had been almost a year since a young cougar had attacked Sam as she rode through Lost Canyon. In nightmares, she still felt the impact against her spine and the yank as the starving cat had pulled her backward, off Strawberry, to the ground.

But when she was awake, she was mostly over it

"It's okay," Sam said. "A cougar's not going to be crashing through the brush." Then, noticing Silly's wide eyes and flaring nostrils, she added, "I guess it could be mustangs."

"They're just excited," Jen said, sounding preoccupied. "Do you think this is far enough? I mean, there's no landslide or anything. I'm sure they can get the herd and riders through here with no trouble."

As Ace and Silly huffed uphill, Sam stopped watching the far peaks, still tipped with snow, and studied the terrain around them. In the underbrush she glimpsed swatches of purple and crimson, but it wasn't until both horses stopped, nostrils quivering, that Sam recognized the wild roses and thistles.

Pretty and unexpected, they were also sharp with thorns and stickers. They'd better make sure the cattle didn't detour for a spiny snack.

"What is it, girl?" Jen asked her horse.

She leaned forward and pressed her cheek against the mare's golden neck, staring in the same direction.

Through knees resting against her saddle, Sam felt Ace draw a deep breath. His black-tinged ears pricked forward and a shiver ran down his neck. He wasn't winded. He was excited.

Suddenly a nicker rang out ahead of them. The trail curved, so they couldn't see the horse, but Ace and Silly answered before the high-pitched sound faded to an echo.

Probably not a mustang, Sam thought. Wild horses were quieter than domesticated ones.

"Maybe one of Mr. Ryden's other hands rode out earlier," Jen said, in a normal tone. She gathered her reins and eased Silly past Ace. "Let's go see."

Insulted that Silly had taken the lead, Ace surged after the palomino. Sam didn't stop him.

Ace slid to a stop just the same, when Silly ducked her head in a half buck.

"Knock it—" Jen's voice broke off in a gasp.

Reining Ace over so she could see past Jen, Sam realized the trail gradually widened as it started downhill again. About a quarter mile away, a beautiful horse stood in the middle of the path. She fidgeted and tossed her head, deciding whether to come uphill and greet the horses that had returned her call.

Alert and cautious, the mare considered the horses and riders. Her chocolate-brown coat shone with good health. Her flaxen mane hung like an ivory shawl over a neck darkened by sweat. Sam tried to guess at her breed, but couldn't. The mare's wide chest and sloping shoulders should make her smooth-gaited and full of stamina.

As Sam studied the horse's dramatic chocolate and cream coloring, she saw signs that the mare had traveled some distance to reach this quiet spot in the mountains.

This was no mustang. From trimmed whiskers to gentle, interested gaze, everything said she'd been cared for, and kindly.

"Hey girly," Jen called, extending her arm, fingers loosely closed over her palm.

The dark mare was no stranger to handheld treats, either. She started up the trail.

A domineering snort stopped her.

The mare wasn't alone.

I might have guessed, Sam thought. As the stallion stepped from the lowest curve in the road, the Phantom's beauty turned away her irritation. Even in the watery yellow light of morning, he looked half-magical, a creature made of bone, sinew, and moon-beams.

Sam sighed just as Jen demanded, "What's he doing here?"

"Like you're surprised he found her before we did," Sam said quietly. She hoped Jen would take the hint and keep her voice down. Each sighting of the Phantom was a gift.

With an easy, ambling gait, the mare approached the silver stallion. The horses' ears flicked a message back and forth, then they both broke into a trot. A few strides later, they accelerated into a long, graceful gait just short of a gallop.

"Listen to her," Jen said.

The mare's hooves struck in a graceful four-beat rhythm. Sam heard the unfamiliar cadence even as the horses ran in step, necks aligned, so that their manes—his silver and hers white gold—billowed back like waves.

All at once, the Phantom's legs reached a little farther and slanted across the mare's path.

"He's trying to cut her off," Jen muttered.

And take her home to his hidden valley, Sam thought.

Instead of letting herself be herded off the open path, though, the mare stopped.

Surprised, the stallion took a few yards to slow to a walk, then arched his neck and, lifting his knees in a proud display, trotted an arc to come back and face her.

Even from this distance, Sam could read the mare's gentle demeanor. She stared at the Phantom with pricked ears. Then she took a step forward and touched his extended muzzle with her own.

Sam smiled. The mare wanted to be friends, but she didn't want to be pushed around. When he drew near enough, she gave his mane a nibble.

"The Phantom's got a new girlfriend," Jen said in a singsong voice.

To Sam, it was no joke. And Jen knew better than to tease about this. If the mare had been wild, that would be one thing. But she wasn't.

Once before the stallion had been accused of stealing domestic mares, but the accusation had proven false. And just last month, Linc Slocum's mare Hotspot had joined the Phantom's herd after she'd escaped from the thief who'd stolen her and her foal.

Where had this glossy, stable-fed beauty come from?

Head high, the silver stallion acted as if he deserved the affectionate nuzzling.

Jen broke Sam's trance by jostling her arm. The movement stirred Ace, too, and he gave a "What's this?" snort.

"We really should go back," Jen said, then added, "No way, Silly."

Jen's amused tone alerted Sam to the palomino's expression. She stared spellbound at the horses on the trail below as if they were performing just for her.

"I know," Sam said.

The stallion must have heard Sam's voice, because he stepped away from the mare's grooming nibbles and stared up the hillside. Sam didn't move, but her heart rejoiced. Just days ago, the Phantom couldn't have heard a thunderclap. Now he recognized her voice and stood waiting for some sign between them.

Zanzibar. Could the stallion's secret name float like a feather on a gust of wind, leaving her mind to drift to the wild stallion's? As if it could, he tossed his heavy mane back and pawed the mountain path.

But then, it was as if Sam had vanished.

The stallion had no more time for humans. The mare beside him must be added to his herd. Now.

This time the stallion flattened his ears. Then he lowered his head and snaked it so close to the mare's mahogany legs, threatening to nip.

For the first time, the mare's ears lay back along her neck and she returned the warning with a clack of her teeth.

Startled, the Phantom looked back over his shoulder, as if she couldn't possibly be snapping at him.

"We really should go, but this is too good," Jen said, covering her lips against a laugh.

Should Sam feel sorry for the stallion?

No, she thought in the next instant. He'd just begun to flirt.

Arching his neck and tucking his chin until it bumped his chest, the Phantom showed off his prance. Then, with ears still laid back, he rocked into a lope. If he could have seen the new-risen sun glinting off the dapples that glittered beneath his hide like silver coins, he would have been even more arrogant.

"It's not going to work," Jen said.

It turned out she was right.

As soon as the Phantom lowered his head again, the mare's ears flattened into her mane and her tail swished in irritation.

Fed up with her stalling, the stallion tried to bully her. His silver shoulder struck her chocolate one. She gave a high pitched squeal before kicking out a hind hoof.

The stallion shied, then circled her at a slow trot.

"I can hear him thinking from here," Jen joked. "He can't believe it. The almighty Phantom's getting the cold shoulder."

Rejection didn't sit well with the silver stallion.

His trot lengthened, and then he was galloping, tightening his circle around the mare. She shifted and gave a nervous nicker. When he heard her uncertainty, the stallion charged.

Was he planning to ram into the mare, push her off the path, and propel her through the brush, back to his herd? If he collided with the mare's hindquarters, she'd have no choice.

The chocolate mare didn't feel like taking his orders.

When two hind hooves lashed out just beneath the stallion's nose, he slid to a stop.

"That woulda hurt," Jen said as the Phantom veered away.

Still moving at a trot, the mustang shook his head, clearing the ropey mane and forelock from his eyes.

"He'll leave," Sam said. "He can't take a chance on being injured."

For the good of the herd, he had to stay strong.

Suddenly, the Phantom wheeled away and crashed into the brush at the side of the trail. The herbal scent of crushed sagebrush filled the air as he stopped and looked back at the reluctant mare. He gave a buck, and powdery soil swirled around him. As the dust cleared, he tilted his head to one side and his mouth was open.

To Sam, he looked playful as a pup.

Follow me and you won't be sorry, he seemed to say.

But the mare couldn't know about the secret green valley with its cold stream and soaring red rock walls. She stood her ground, watching him.

Giving arrogance one last try, the Phantom rose into a rear. His strong front legs struck at the air.

How could she resist? Sam wondered.

But she did. The chocolate-brown mare was not impressed with the silver stallion's rearing strength.

"Smart girl," Jen said.

When he came back to earth, the stallion stood still. He might have been carved from white quartz as he waited.

But the mare looked right through him.

Finally, without a flicker of interest in Sam or Ace, the Phantom trotted away, forcing a path through a crackling thicket of wild roses.

Read all the Phantom Stallion books!

AVON BOOKS
An Imprint of HarperCollins Publishers

www.phantomstallion.com
www.harperteen.com